Edward Upward was born in 1903 at Romford, Essex, and educated at Repton and at Corpus Christi College, Cambridge, where he read English and History, and was awarded the Chancellor's Medal for English Verse. While at Cambridge he created with Christopher Isherwood a series of stories about the fictitious village of Mortmere. After graduating he became a schoolmaster; from 1931 until his retirement in 1961 he taught at Alleyn's School, Dulwich, where he was a housemaster and head of the English department.

Edward Upward's first novel, *Journey to the Border*, was originally published by Leonard and Virginia Woolf at the Hogarth Press in 1938. In the 1930s he also contributed articles to *New Country, New Writing* and the *Left Review* and was on the editorial board of *The Ploughshare*, journal of the Teachers' Anti-War Movement. For sixteen years he was a member of the Communist Party of Great Britain, but he left it in 1948 because he believed it was ceasing to be a Marxist party.

Between 1942 and 1961 Upward wrote nothing, mainly for political reasons, but in 1962 Heinemann published *In the Thirties*, the first part of his trilogy of novels *The Spiral Ascent*. The second part, *The Rotten Elements*, and the third, *No Home but the Struggle*, were published in 1969 and 1977. Edward Upward's other books include *The Railway Accident and Other Stories* (1969), *The Night Walk and Other Stories* (1987), and in the current Enitharmon series, *An Unmentionable Man* and *The Mortmere Stories*.

Since 1962 Edward Upward and his wife have lived at Sandown in the Isle of Wight. They have a son and a daughter and four grandsons.

EDWARD UPWARD
Journey to the Border

INTRODUCED BY STEPHEN SPENDER

London
ENITHARMON PRESS
1994

First published in 1994
by the Enitharmon Press
36 St George's Avenue
London N7 0HD

Distributed in Europe
by Password (Books) Ltd.
23 New Mount Street
Manchester, M4 4DE

Distributed in the USA
by Dufour Editions Inc.
PO Box 449, Chester Springs
Pennsylvania 19425

ISBN 1 870612 59 0 (paper)
ISBN 1 870612 74 4 (cloth)

This is a revised version of the novel first
published by Leonard and Virginia Woolf
at the Hogarth Press in 1938.

The paperback edition comprises 1000 copies;
the cloth edition, limited to 50 copies,
is signed by Edward Upward and Stephen Spender.

The text of *Journey to the Border* is set in
10pt Times by Bryan Williamson, Frome, Somerset
and printed by
The Cromwell Press, Melksham, Wiltshire

BOOKS BY EDWARD UPWARD

Journey to the Border (Hogarth Press, 1938)

*

THE SPIRAL ASCENT: A Trilogy
In the Thirties (Heinemann, 1962)
The Rotten Elements (Heinemann, 1969)
No Home but the Struggle (Heinemann, 1977)

The Spiral Ascent was also published in one
volume by Heinemann in 1977, and reissued in three
paperback volumes by Quartet in 1978-79.

*

The Railway Accident and Other Stories (Heinemann, 1969;
Penguin, 1972 and 1988)
The Night Walk and Other Stories (Heinemann, 1987)

*

Journey to the Border – a revised version (Enitharmon, 1994)
introduced by Stephen Spender

An Unmentionable Man (Enitharmon, 1994)
introduced by Frank Kermode

with Christopher Isherwood
The Mortmere Stories (Enitharmon, 1994)
introduced by Katherine Bucknell

Introduction

I see the novelist Edward Upward as a voyager on this earth who is extremely aware of its ills but at the same time has never lost his faith that its inhabitants – some of them at least – have the power to create a better world: one of social justice, affection and the life of the imagination.

This journey is essentially religious. But Upward is a rationalist accepting scientific truth and rejecting the superstitions of institutionalised religion.

His fiction tends to take the form of the journey or quest by a protagonist who, thinly disguised, and in altered circumstances, is, under various fictitious names, the author himself. He is an idiosyncratic observer who combines a caricaturist's vision of upper and middle-class English society with a developing belief in the workers and the oppressed. After an initial surrealistic phase, he is political in that he interprets the world as a struggle between those whose values are those of their own property, power and self-interest, and those who share the vision of a world which might be transformed in the interests of the whole community. After a period of distrust and a certain class-coyness (rather than class-consciousness) he decides that these values are to be found among the workers.

In being a writer with a social vision Upward fits into a category of novelists in this century, narrators of their own journey on the planet Earth, who reject the existing social order, which they find to be unjust, and go in search of some achievable materialistic and social Utopia. He is in the tradition of Samuel Butler in *Erewhon*, H.G. Wells in his early novels, but, stylistically, with the influence of early James Joyce thrown in.

Yet the 1930s' background of *Journey to the Border* is an England more neurotic than that in which Butler and Wells were writing. These people whom the tutor meets in a tent during the races are the last generation of empire builders, the types whom Auden invokes in his Airman's Journal in *The Orators*, the neurotic upper and middle-class inhabitants of 'England, this country of ours where no one is well.'

One of the caricatured 'types' whom the tutor meets in the tent is Mavors – the psychological Healer, based perhaps on the psychologist Homer Lane whose ideas at one time influenced the young Auden. In trying to persuade the tutor that his feelings about the evils of modern society are symptoms of the tutor's own neurosis which can only be healed by cultivating the inner calls of Desire, Mavors confronts the tutor with a vision of the contemporary world which, he argues, the tutor, in the interests of Desire, must reject. But this picture conveys much of the horror of the world as it looked to Upward's generation in the 1930s – with poverty, unemployment, the rise of Hitler and the threat of war:

> 'You will diagnose poverty, malnutrition, overcrowding, injustice and crime. And now reason will come into its own. It will show you a future black with horror, will prove beyond dispute that there can be no escape, that conditions must steadily worsen, unrest grow, starvation and tyranny advance, and finally that war will deluge the whole world with blood.'

This is, indeed, how the world looked to the young writers of the Thirties, who proved to be more truthful prophets than the politicians in the democratic countries of that era.

However in *Journey to the Border* Upward is by no means a case of the writer whose insights have been overtaken by events which proved them to be true. He is also a visionary of wonderful language and extraordinary power. If one can call visions biting, his are when he describes the objects of his contempt – the tutor's employers, for instance, and the people who raise their hands in the fascist salute in the tent. But he is also the poet of visions which, although they fit within the context of his politics, seem to transcend time and their occasion like pure poetry.

8

There stands out from these pages the description of the steam-roller, in the passage beginning:

> It was simple and bold and powerful, crested in front with a rampant brass unicorn, thumping with its pistons like a thumping heart.

I need quote no more because the reader will find the whole long and wonderfully sustained passage in this text. This is prose poetry. And it is not too much to say that *Journey to the Border* contains some of the most beautiful prose poems of the century.

STEPHEN SPENDER
London, March 1994

1

Ever since breakfast the tutor had been preparing to tell Mr Parkin that he would rather not accompany him and the boy to the races. 'Why should I?' he thought. 'I may have been forced to sell myself as a purveyor of the kind of trash that's required for a public school Common Entrance examination but this doesn't mean I'm going to act as a footman as well.' He was standing at the window of the dining-room, waiting for Mr Parkin to come downstairs. The pure-bred terrier puppy lay weakly outside in the sun, muzzle on paws, watching the chaffinches pick up bits of monkey-nut from the gravel drive. The boy had got tired of experimentally dropping very thin shavings of nut into the tadpole jar on the window-sill, and had probably gone off to the garage to fool round and irritate the chauffeur. Soon his father would become anxious and start shouting for him from upstairs.

'Presumably after three months of this I've a right to a few hours' leisure,' the tutor thought with fury. He quickly checked the feeling. The important thing was to remember what he had discovered at breakfast. Going from the table to the sideboard in order to avoid implicating himself in the advice which Mr Parkin had been giving the boy against over-excitement at the races, he had felt for the first time since his arrival that he wanted to spend a day at this house. On previous mornings the gilt and white dining-room with its window view of an artificial lake, fir trees, lawns, huge flowerbeds, had suggested nothing to him except that he was wasting his life in a faked and isolated world incompletely retrieved from the eighteenth century, but today the unpleasant prospect of standing about for hours in a field and of meeting the cheerful MacCreath girls or Humphrey Silcox the ship-owner's son had inversely reflected a fictitious value over everything unconnected with the races. The lake, the four lawns all at different levels, the blue stable clock, pigeons, the whitish-green sword-like leaves of the irises, even the scalloped ivory knob of the silver-plated chafing-dish on the sideboard, had seemed to offer possibilities of enjoyment which at all costs he must not fail to follow up.

What he would do here if he managed to escape the races had been and still was uncertain, but it would be something important and at the same time deliberately strange, some act which would violently break the continuity of his life as a hired tutor. It might be a bogus ceremony of purification, performed in the kitchen or in the stable loft or under the dining-room table or on the croquet lawn. He would symbolically wash off all the dismal servilities of the past three months. He might even climb a fir tree, or go for a forty-mile bicycle ride, or drop one of the boy's exercise books into the lake, or simply peer in through the broken pane of the outhouse where the electricity was made. And the interesting point, as he now began to realize, was that whatever form the act might eventually take it wouldn't be altogether a farce. It would be something more than a frantic and temporary reaction against three months of self-effacement. Yes, it would be the beginning of a new technique, a first step towards solving the problem of how to live in this house.

Standing at the dining-room window he became aware that his valuation of the Parkins had hitherto been quite inadequate: he had disliked them because he had wrongly taken them, not for freaks belonging to the same order of reality as the characters in a Grimm's fairy story or a cinema film, but for ordinary living people. Instead of recognizing their oddity, and of using it as a pretext for being equally odd himself, he had inexcusably stood on his dignity, suspected petty insults, tried to think of stinging retorts. But in future he would be quite different. From this morning on he would be as fantastic, as expansively imaginative, as he liked. He would do just what he liked. More than that, he would do it in such a way that no one would realize he was doing it: they would merely think that he was at last settling down to country life. He saw it clearly now – he would pretend to be one of them. He would wear a check cap, borrow the boy's fishing-rod, examine rabbit-holes, shoot at bats from his bedroom window with an air pistol. He would be invulnerable. Never again would he have to be on the defensive. He would see the house in a new light, would want to live here, would even choose to live here rather than elsewhere. It would have become the sole place, perhaps in the world, where he could get just this kind of pleasure.

There was one imminent danger, however. He might be tricked into a sordid quarrel with Mr Parkin about the races. He mightn't find it easy to put the new technique into operation straight away. In fact it was precisely this uncertainty which made it all the more essential for him to have the day free for thinking out the technique in detail. That was why he couldn't submit to going to the races. But an emotional scene with Mr Parkin might poison the whole morning. Not only that – it might disenchant the tutor with the new technique altogether. 'No,' he decided, 'I've got to begin to learn to control myself. Hysteria, however impressive, merely puts me at the mercy of these people.'

If Mr Parkin, who was now coming down the stairs after leaving his wife's bedroom, had been aware of what the tutor had just decided he would have been doubly surprised. He not only had no suspicion that the tutor wasn't perfectly contented in his house, but he had always regarded him as a rather frigid little man. Rather too unresponsive to be an entirely suitable companion for the boy. It wasn't that the Agency had recommended a tutor who hadn't the manners of a gentleman – and after all there was a very real risk of that happening nowadays – but Mr Parkin would have preferred, or imagined he would have preferred, someone more sympathetic and at the same time capable of exercising a stricter discipline. Actually, though he didn't realize it, no sort of tutor would have satisfied him. Fussing about the boy had been, along with midday drinking at a small hotel in the company of well-to-do local farmers, his chief interest since he had given up playing at farming ten years before. Even this morning, in spite of counter-excitement at the prospect of the races, he had chosen to open a nagging discussion with his wife about making the boy wear two scarves in the car – a detail on which they were really agreed from the start.

'Above all, no fireworks,' the tutor warned himself. Mr Parkin had stopped for a moment outside the dining-room door. He shouted up to his wife: 'I'll tell Stokes to bring the plaid rug.' She screamed an unintelligible answer. He peered round the door.

'You here?'

The corner of his mouth gave a suspicious twitch, exposing a blackened premolar tooth. He came into the room.

'Where's the boy?'

'I think he went to the garage.'

'I don't want him playing about with that motor-mower.'

Surprisingly Mr Parkin made no further comment. Wincing a little, he limped over to the window, supporting himself on the way by sliding a clenched hand along the edge of the table. His swollen knee was evidently painful this morning – as it perversely always was now whenever there seemed a chance of his getting a day's sport of any kind. But no doubt he was able to compensate himself with the theory that the swelling was hereditary. He had often proudly told the boy that he, too, when the time came, would develop the same trouble as his father and grandfather before him. The tutor had wondered whether the trouble might simply have been due, in both cases, to gonorrhoea.

'That's a nasty thing to do,' Mr Parkin suddenly said.

'What?'

'Look at it.'

He pointed to the tadpole jar on the window-sill. The tutor noticed that the boy had dropped into it not only thin shavings of nut, but also bits of shell.

'I didn't know he had done that. I'm sorry.'

'It's mucky.' But Mr Parkin felt, in view of the tutor's apology, that he was going too far. He became affectedly thoughtful: 'I can't help thinking that some change has come over Donald lately. He always used to be such a neat-minded boy.'

'Perhaps it's due to his illness.'

'No, I don't feel it's that. Naturally that makes him a bit feckless at times, poor chap. But he's become so untidy during these last few months. His mother and I can't account for it at all.'

'It certainly is rather extraordinary.'

Half smiling, half doubtful whether his remarks had gone home, Mr Parkin nodded. An involuntary nervous tremor gave a mock obsequiousness to the downward movement of his head. His red-rimmed, slightly bloodshot eyes fixed the tutor for a moment, then glanced out of the window. He abruptly, almost violently, asked:

'Hasn't Stokes come round to fetch the hamper yet?'

'I don't think so.'

'I wonder what the devil's happened now. It's going to be bad enough not having the Daimler today. It's a confounded nuisance he didn't discover there was something wrong with it yesterday evening. I'd be glad to know how he imagines he's going to get four of us into the Austin. We'll have our legs knocked to pieces with that damned hamper on top of us. I suppose he's forgotten all about that.'

Mr Parkin's irritation, which he would never have indulged if he'd been speaking to Stokes in person, seemed to be directed chiefly against the tutor.

'If Mrs Parkin is going with you perhaps it would be more comfortable for her if I didn't come in the car,' the tutor said. 'I could ask Donald to lend me his bicycle.'

'Mrs Parkin isn't going with us.'

'But I thought you said there would be four in the car.'

'Quite right. I did. And with Stokes there'll be five.'

Mr Parkin smilingly declined to offer any explanation.

The tutor was confused, remarked insincerely:

'I hope Mrs Parkin is better this morning.'

'Well, I can't say she is. She's about the same.'

'I'm sorry.'

'Of course, as you know, it's only what is to be expected at her time of life. All women have to go through it when they reach a certain age. Just like horses. You know what I mean.'

'I see.'

'That's all it is. It's only what's to be expected.'

Watching the tutor's face, Mr Parkin added:

15

'Naturally, she doesn't want to go with the whole crowd of us in the small car just at present.'

'No, I suppose not,' the tutor said. 'As a matter of fact I was thinking that if someone else were going in the car instead of Mrs Parkin, then, perhaps, all the same, it might be more convenient if I didn't come with you.'

'I don't advise you to try to get to the races on a bicycle. You'd find yourself in for a longer ride than you think.'

'But, surely, if the car will be uncomfortable for you –'

'Pah, I was almost ashamed to invite MacCreath to come with us when he rang up this morning. But what else could I do? His wife's going to the dentist and she wants the Bentley and those daughters of his have had the cheek to drive off for the day in the two-seater – with friends from London,' Mr Parkin sneered. 'Caw – a couple of them were over here in the garden last year. They couldn't bear seeing anyone picking up worms, they said. The stuck-up effeminate young puppies. I could have slashed them across the faces with a whip.'

The tutor, conscious that Mr Parkin's anger was not altogether retrospective, said casually:

'If Mr MacCreath's coming I might as well stay here and leave room for him in the car.'

Mr Parkin stared at the tutor with excessive surprise.

'Why, of course not. That won't be necessary at all.'

'But I'd really prefer spending the day here.'

'Absurd. How do you suppose you'd get anything to eat?'

'I can get it at a pub. I was thinking of going for a walk.'

'There's no need to do that. Everything has been arranged for you to come with us.'

Mr Parkin's tone of voice was insultingly soothing, almost sing-song. The tutor flushed, was on the point of retorting that he wasn't in the least interested in the races. But he remembered that he must be very careful. The new technique. He mustn't feel angry. And almost immediately Mr Parkin added:

'Mind you, I don't want to hinder you in any way if you'd prefer going for a walk. But it seems rather unreasonable to choose the one day when you've a chance to go to the races.' Mr Parkin smiled slightly. 'Surely any other day would do just as well. Why

16

not tomorrow? As soon as Donald has gone off to church. I'm only too glad that you *want* to get out into the country for a bit.'

The tutor stared coldly out of the window.

'That's to say' – Mr Parkin was suggestive – 'unless you've definite plans for meeting someone today.'

The tutor wavered.

'No,' he admitted. 'I haven't.'

He felt at once he had made a mistake. Mr Parkin was contemptuously triumphant:

'Well, then, you don't want to miss the races, do you?'

The tutor didn't answer. He wondered whether he ought to have lied about meeting someone. Perhaps he ought to have suggested that he was going whoring. Any lie would have served, the more startling the better. He must never forget that he was dealing with a moneyed imbecile. Nothing could be more degrading than to tell Mr Parkin the truth. But after all the tutor had not told him the truth. He had not made a mistake. He had been right to give the impression that he had surrendered. Because he would take good care to contradict the impression at the very last moment. He would be frankly irresponsible. He would run away, go to bed, hide himself in the kitchen garden, jump out of the car, vanish, escape anyhow. Perhaps it might have been better still if he had consented outright to going to the races. That would have been even more in keeping with the new technique. Up to the very last minute he would have pretended to be delighted by Mr Parkin's generosity in offering him a seat in the car. He would have chatted enthusiastically about the races. He would have got all the facts about the horses out of the newspapers, would have appeared to be an expert, would have known far more about the races than anyone else in the house. Then, just as Mr Parkin and the boy were stepping into the car, he would unaccountably have walked off into the kitchen garden. Would he? Would he do it now? And even if he did, even if these proposed antics weren't just desperate fantasies, even if he lay flat on the drive and refused to be moved, did he want to behave like this? Was it good, did he prefer these contortions, the elfish independence of an ill-treated child, to the ordinary satisfaction of everyday wishes, did he choose the equilibrium of madness, would he rather tell lies, was it even necessary?

Mr Parkin stood grinning, gratified by the tutor's awkwardness. He grinned like a panting collie-dog. His head nodded jerkily, his mouth hung open, his tongue quivered. A look of spiteful cunning crossed his face. There were small pockmarks in the shaven flesh round the corners of his mouth beneath the points of his moustache. The conversation with the tutor had stimulated him, toned up his nerves.

It was not necessary. The tutor was not destitute, not driven to trickery by poverty, Mr Parkin held no whip, was not a feudal serf-owner or a public school prefect, could not punish or coerce him. His three months' surrender to Mr Parkin had been due to nothing but cowardice. Why hadn't he at the start insisted that he should have at least one hour every day off duty, away from the boy? Mere weakness: and soon he had begun to justify his weakness by pretending that servility was inevitable, a necessary condition of modern life, that it would have been the same or worse anywhere else, that he would be petty or romantic if he attempted to gain any concession from Mr Parkin. The new technique was simply the latest phase of this pretence, the most frantic cowardice of all. It was a day-dream victory. He had surrendered to Mr Parkin. To an ignorant snob who couldn't spell properly, who regarded himself as an old English Squire, who held theories about women and about servants which would have seemed out of date even to the editor of a stunt newspaper.

Mr Parkin had suddenly noticed something on the sideboard. His grin changed to an absurd pout of fury. He fumbled in one of the pockets of his waistcoat, brought out a small key. He limped over to the sideboard. The tantalus had been left unlocked. He looked briefly at the tutor and saw that the tutor was smiling. He hesitated, lost control, spoke:

'Some drunken devil has been stealing the brandy again.'

His face relaxed instantly, became placid. It was greasy and sallow as though he had been rubbing olive oil into it. He bent down, brought out another key, opened the sideboard wine cupboard. The tutor watched him with hatred. 'This well-fed swine,' he thought. A swine, a swine who had never doubted his power

18

to impose his trivial swinish standards on everyone in the house. And who had had no reason to doubt it. Who poisoned the whole district. Who succeeded in making the farm labourers play up to his conception of them as simple rustic toadies. Who bribed the cobbler and the grocer with whisky to come and consult him about their family troubles. Who despised the village school-master as an upstart earning far too large a salary. Whose power extended even beyond the district, touched London, could buy up an expensively educated young man at any time to dance attendance on his boy. But the tutor had been something more than a mere obedient attendant, a mere passive jumping dummy. It was no good day-dreaming that he had been perse-cuted by an ineluctable Power. If he had been compelled with whips, dragged into the workroom every morning and made to teach Latin and Scripture at the point of a rook rifle, kicked into church every Sunday, forcibly hustled into a dinner jacket by the butler or the contemptuous Scottish chambermaid every evening – then he might have been able to forgive himself. But the truth was that long before any pressure had been brought to bear on him he had deliberately chosen to be a lackey, had been active, not passive, had almost fallen over himself in his shy hurry to comply with what he assumed the Parkins wanted. No one had told him to teach Latin and Scripture or to wear a dinner jacket or to take the boy to church. He had done these things because he had guessed that Mr Parkin thought they were good for the boy – and consequently Mr Parkin had felt quite safe in boasting that he himself regarded Latin as a waste of time and religion as worse than useless to people who could go straight without it. The tutor had consented to traffic in hypocrisies which even Mr Parkin was glad not to have to dirty his hands with. He had catered for the meanest uncertainties of a reactionary snob. He had been useful to Mr Parkin rather as a police spy is to a bishop, relieved him of a doubtful job, and now Mr Parkin was able to adopt the pretence of not being in the least responsible for the sort of education the boy was getting and to give the boy the impression that it was a sham imposed on both of them by an impecuniously genteel scholastic hack.

Watching Mr Parkin lift out and examine bottles from the

wine cupboard, the tutor for a moment suspected himself of exaggerating. How could a person of intelligence take anything that happened in this household seriously? Instantly the tutor repudiated the question, condemned it as a relic of his worst cowardice. His contemptible pose of detachment, trying to see himself as a cynical observer, someone perfectly disguised as a hired tutor but really far far different, altogether inscrutable. Viler still, his attempt to pretend that the Parkins were not quite living people, were modern goblins, unbelievable freaks to be amusingly described in amazing letters to his friends. And he had imagined that these childish deceits preserved his independence, his integrity. As though his nature would have received some subtle everlasting stain if he had once admitted to himself that he was a tutor in an ordinary country house. The horror of being subdued to what he worked in, like the dyer's hand. But it was just his hand, his body, his real life, his leisure which he had allowed to be subdued. While his nature, the soul for which he had been so meanly alarmed, had performed its invisible fairy-story acrobatics, he had smiled daily at table, agreed with everything the Parkins had said, drunk their beer, obeyed their orders, given up his whole time to the boy. Any effort to assert himself in practice he would have considered degrading, petty, a danger to his soul. But he had failed even to save his soul. Its wilful fairy stories were no more than twisted images of his real predicament. He had failed, prostituted himself deliberately in every way. He had wasted in trivialities and dishonesties his one and only life, his life which might have been so full of, so bright with, so ardent for – what? Oh, wonders: love and knowledge and creation, history, science, poetry, interesting daily work, holidays, joy. He had voluntarily thrown all those away.

For the sake of snugness, for beer at lunch and dinner, for early morning tea and a bright bedroom with a view of rooks' nests among the tree-tops, for the sake of preserving a small private room in his mind to which he could always retire and in which he could pose as an intellectual experimenter, for the hope of holding a job which was after all less strenuous and less likely to encroach on his imaginary leisure than most other jobs. He had preserved nothing. He had become a mule, a eunuch, quite sexless, too listless even to kick. But there was going to be a change. Suddenly. A flash, a concentration of revulsion, an insurrection of the nerves, a Leviathan of fury turning over in the black ocean of apathy. He would tell Mr Parkin what he thought about country life and racing. Now. Instantly.

A large saloon car, grinding the gravel, spitting small stones from beneath its semi-balloon tyres, passed by the window and drew up outside the front door.

Mr Parkin shut the door of the wine cupboard and stood up. He smiled with pleasure.

'That's MacCreath,' he said.

Now. Quick.

But MacCreath was quicker than the tutor. The rooks, scattering from the trees at the sound of the car, were quicker. The boy, racing across the lawn from the garage, treading down the crocuses between the trees, shouting 'Uncle Hamish', waving a fishing-rod, was quicker. To defy Mr Parkin now would be merely theatrical. The tutor's resolution had become a dream from which he had been jerked awake by the ordinary noises of the daytime. Defiance would be as ridiculous as rushing down to breakfast in pyjamas and shouting, 'Shut the greenhouse door against the tarantula', or 'What have you done with my dancing-girl?' And already MacCreath was standing in the room, saying with the smoothest cordiality:

'Good morning, Jim. Looks as if we are going to have a beautiful day for it this time.'

'Yes, it looks like it,' Mr Parkin said cautiously, controlling his excitement.

MacCreath directed a very amiable nod of greeting towards the tutor. The boy lunged into the room, followed by the frisking terrier puppy.

'Steady, steady,' Mr Parkin snarled. 'Do you want to smash up the whole house?'

'I haven't smashed anything,' the boy said pertly.

Mr Parkin exploded: 'If you're going to fool about and get over-excited you're not coming with us to the races. We don't want you laid up for months in the house with a strained heart.'

The boy, though he didn't believe that his father would stop him going to the races, was temporarily cowed by the words.

MacCreath changed the subject: 'Well, how are the lessons going, Donald?'

'Oh, all right.'

Outside, MacCreath's chauffeur had turned the car and was repassing the window. Mr Parkin looked at his watch.

'I can't think what's making Stokes so late. I shall have to ring him up.'

He went out into the hall.

No one would compel the tutor to get into the car. Even now he needn't go to the races. He had only to stand still at the window of the dining-room and watch the others go into the car. Or suppose they spoke to him and asked why he wasn't coming. He needn't answer. Then probably they would ring up a doctor. But why shouldn't he tell them frankly that he intended to stay here? Why hadn't he told them? Because of MacCreath. Because MacCreath was a gentleman. Because he was smooth-spoken and had a sportsman's open-air complexion and was wearing an unassertive tweed overcoat and a milky-tea-coloured shirt and collar. But that was just why the tutor ought to speak out, ought to slash out, to rip to shreds this Philistine's cocksure affability.

In reality MacCreath was not cocksure. He was quite aware of the tutor's hostility. And he partly understood it. He wanted to say something which would show that he wasn't as unintelligent as Mr Parkin, that in spite of being a friend of Mr Parkin's he regarded him as a bit of a joke. But the tutor was inaccessible, frigidly avoided his glances. MacCreath spoke to the boy instead.

'I shouldn't put your face too close to the dog's if I were you.'

'Why? Ronald's quite clean. Aren't you, Ronald? Eh, boy? Haven't you a nice clean wet kisser?'

'Well, I shouldn't do it. You never know what germs a dog mayn't pick up.' MacCreath added a generalization in the friendly hope of drawing some remark from the tutor: 'It's a strange thing that the better bred a dog is the more he'll poke his nose into any filth he comes across.'

'Yes,' the tutor said mechanically.

MacCreath wasn't offended. He appeared not to have expected

any further comment. His attention tactfully strayed to the door. Mr Parkin could be heard telephoning: 'and bring the plaid rug.' MacCreath smiled. He seemed to appeal, to be on the point of asking serio-comically: 'Did you ever hear anything like it?' But his gentlemanly clothes, his insinuating good humour, the soft confident aggression of his voice whenever he spoke, contradicted this impression. And actually he asked:

'Are you going to the dance at the town hall this evening?'

'I don't know.'

'My little girls would be very glad to see you there.'

The tutor was surprised. He had imagined that people like MacCreath would want to guard their daughters against young men without money. But MacCreath was almost apologizing for bringing his daughters to the tutor's notice. Was this humility simply a trick, a super-politeness designed to be so overwhelming in its condescension that the tutor would automatically give up all thoughts of going to the dance?

'It ought to be quite a good show,' MacCreath said. 'No evening dress, of course.'

'I don't know whether I shall be able to get away.'

'I hope you will.'

Again the suggestion of diffidence. As though MacCreath doubted whether the tutor would want to go to a dance at which no one wore evening dress.

'By the way, do you play bridge?' MacCreath asked.

'No.'

The tutor was startled at the effect of his abruptness. For the first time MacCreath looked hurt. His smile weakened to a meek weariness, his forehead wrinkled helplessly. He seemed to have lost all his confidence, to be incapable even of resentment. A suspicion occurred to the tutor: perhaps MacCreath wasn't really at all sure of himself, wasn't sure that he could pass as a gentleman. Perhaps he hadn't been to a public school, had sold newspapers on the streets of Glasgow, owed his present position solely to his wife's money. Perhaps his good humour, his tolerance, his popularity at the golf club, with the local farmers, with servants, with the Parkins, were due not to any sense of power but to the sense of a weakness in his social armour. Worse,

23

perhaps he regarded the tutor as a gentleman, even admired him, was trying to adapt himself to him.

On the floor the boy was playing with the puppy. One of his stockings had slipped down to his ankle, exposing a flabby white leg.

'We're brothers, we are. Yes, Ronald, yes. Come on, say yes. You're human, aren't you? What's my name?' The puppy yapped. 'My name's Donald. Quite right. Well done. Now don't forget it. Ronald, Donald. We're brothers, we are.'

On the shiny flesh of the boy's calf, bulging from pressure against the carpet, the tutor noticed a soft brown mole. He had an impulse to kick the leg. If MacCreath hadn't been there he would probably have said something spiteful to the boy about the puppy. And MacCreath, almost as if he had been aware of the tutor's childish irritation, seemed to recover, to regain confidence. He asked the boy teasingly:

'You don't really believe he can understand what you're saying, do you?'

'Of course he can. Dogs are human beings.'

'That's not saying much for human beings.'

The boy looked puzzled. MacCreath couldn't forbear trying to catch the tutor's eye. Soon he would speak to him again, make another advance. Not assertively or revengefully, not humbly or forgivingly, but comfortably and with good humour. His blue-grey eyes, shallow and shiny as though they had been painted on bits of talc, would fix the tutor's with a temperate semi-blind stare. He would accept the tutor. Just as, after the initial shock, he would possibly have accepted a theft or a sexual indiscretion if one had been committed in his presence. Just as he accepted the boasters and drunks at the golf club or the respectable farmers and the village postman at the pub. His weakness was that he could never in any circumstances feel sufficiently secure to be able to reject the actual. His strength was that he felt comfortable enough to be able to eject a cloud-screen of tolerant kindliness against anything angular or rebellious. That accounted for his popularity. He would not be in favour of a surgical operation. But suppose the operation wasn't really necessary, suppose after all the abscess was nothing more than a pustule. What if the tutor, not MacCreath, was contemptibly in the wrong? Wasn't it possible that the tutor had become a social hypochondriac, that his isolation in this house had made him over-introspective, psychologic, almost unbalanced, ridiculously ready to see the habits of the Parkins and their friends and servants as all-important horrors? Was anything that happened in this house worth going to extremes about?

No one sane could regard Mr Parkin as a dangerous power. He was a weakness – freakishly sprouting in the accidental manure of his inherited money. He was childish, quite as excited as his son about the races. Perhaps more excited. He came in from the hall carrying an aluminium shooting stick, his nostrils twitching, his eyes wide open. He seemed on the point of making a tremendous statement.

'Stokes will be round in a couple of minutes,' he said. 'Then the music begins in earnest.'

At once he started laughing. MacCreath joined him. They were trying to control themselves and failing wildly. They were like young girls with a daring secret. What was it all about? Probably a horse they had backed – or they might for some reason be laughing at the tutor. He didn't know and hadn't the energy to think it out.

MacCreath was the first to recover. 'It's a shame Monica can't come. It would do her good.'

'Well it might, but I think she's wise not to take any risks.'

Mr Parkin was probably going to explain again that it was just like horses, but the boy interrupted him with a dutiful whine:

'I'm so sorry for poor Mummy.'

And why dutiful? There was no reason for thinking the boy wasn't sincere. In fact, the hypocrisy and the whine were simply another hypochondriacal delusion of the tutor's. He must be slightly unwell. This house must have tainted his nerves, made him narrow, venomous, dehumanized him. MacCreath's attitude towards the Parkins wasn't morbid, though it might be complacent. Mr Parkin might be a fool but he wasn't the medieval devil that the tutor had imagined. The boy was an ordinary boy, rather spoiled by his mother. The races would be boring, but they wouldn't be the end of the world.

25

Already the car could be heard coming up the drive. What would the tutor gain by bursting out into diseased heroics? The races wouldn't be altogether loathsome. That idea had been a delusion due to his tainted nerves. Nothing that happened while he was with the Parkins could be in the least frightful or important. Therefore he must kill the nerves, put an end to feeling. He must mechanically follow Mr Parkin and MacCreath out of the room and into the hall.

He was already following them. Mr Parkin, limping, recklessly digging his shooting-stick into the carpet, paused a moment, asked MacCreath whether he would like a drink. MacCreath said that his doctor had ordered him to go on the water-cart. Mr Parkin was amazed. The tutor stared glassily into the hall. Someone had fetched his overcoat for him and put it over the back of an antique chair. He picked it up. His nerves were dead. He was as nerveless as the sandwiches in the hamper which the butler was carrying through the hall to the front door. He had killed feeling, because feeling had been diseased. He felt nothing except a slight flatulence. The hall was only a hall, not a lethal chamber. The two copper warming-pans, the oak barometer, the brass-handled drawers of the huge tallboy, the grandfather clock with moon and stars across its face, the oil painting of bottle-green waves towering against an ochre lighthouse, the brilliantly white circular skylight above the stairs – were not in any way ominous or detestable. They were what they were, and all feelings about them were only feelings. But from now on there would be no more feelings.

He followed Mr Parkin and MacCreath and the boy out of the front door. There was a prolonged far-away ringing in his ear. The butler was lifting the hamper into the car. Mrs Parkin, clutching a quilt to the bosom of her nightdress, leant out over her window-box of daffodils, smiling. Stokes, uniformed, gaitered and gauntleted, looked discreetly sardonic. Holding open the back door of the car he detained Mr Parkin a moment after MacCreath and the boy had stepped inside.

'About that horse, sir.'

'Fritillary?'

'Yes, sir.' Stokes was impressive: 'He may not run today, sir.'

Mr Parkin, one foot on the running-board, writhed as though he had been struck lightly across the calves with a cane.

'Why?'

'I've had information, sir.'

Stokes prepared to shut the door. Mr Parkin wanted to resist, but his legs appeared to disobey him. He got into the car. He had the stunned air of a savage who has been told that an enemy has stolen one of his toe-nail parings. But he couldn't bear to let Stokes go without saying something more to him, however irrelevant. Just as the door was closing he said:

'You'll remember to come round again this evening with the emulsion?'

'Of course, sir.'

'I think my knee is a little worse this evening.'

'I'm sorry to hear that, sir.'

Stokes shut the door. Getting into the driving seat he side-glanced knowingly at the tutor. The tutor sat down beside him. Mrs Parkin waved a fat-wristed hand from the bedroom window above the box of daffodils. The car turned and made up the drive towards the gates. Stokes sat rigid as an idol at the steering-wheel. Outside the gates he changed gear with the minimum of movement, his hand stealthy on the gear lever, his foot on the clutch pedal hinging gently from the ankle. At a sharp bend in the road a wall of dark fir-trees made a temporary mirror of the windscreen, showed him pug-nosed, hemisphere-eyed, faintly grinning with mumbo-jumbo insolence. He *was* an idol. The Parkins depended on him, thought him infallible. He was their doctor, their adviser. He had invented an emulsion and a car polish, and Mr Parkin believed that he could have been a rich man if he'd wanted to. Above all, Mr Parkin was impressed by his memory: when he went shopping he never forgot any of the orders Mrs Parkin had given him, and he never had to write them down. Mr Parkin once, after sneering at education, said of him to the tutor: 'Stokes never had any education, not more than two years at the outside – and look at him now; he could wipe the floor with both of us.' Stokes was the real ruler of this household, the tutor thought. A kind of lay Rasputin, without, so far as the tutor knew, Rasputin's expensive vices.

What trash. Theorizing again. As the car, riding between beech hedges across the huge landscape, wove its sheltered equable hum, so the brain wove its neat private opinions and theories in an immense unconsidered wilderness. The ringing in the tutor's ear grew louder. Any opinion, any theory, was as good or as bad as another. Think of Mr Parkin as a devil or a devil-worshipper or a hero – it didn't matter. Thinking was only an exercise, a weaving of decorations. You looked through the windscreen and saw something and thought 'beech hedges', and imagined they were brown, but you might just as well think 'parrots', and imagine they were black. You looked and saw the miles of country and a river and you thought 'the North of England', but you might as well think 'Switzerland'. Hence the futility of all travel. Why go to Switzerland and say 'mountains' when you can just as easily say 'mountains' here and now? Why go anywhere, why *be* anywhere? You look through the windscreen now and you think – 'There is a river, there are corrugated iron roofs of farm buildings, there farther off is a mining town, there very far off a harbour, there the road reaches the top of a hill' – but all these names are only mental decorations foisted by you and other 'thinkers' upon a non-human world which, but for your interference, would have had no names. Can this hill think or feel or speak, can it say 'I am Belstreet Hill', can it even say 'I am *something*?' It cannot even say that. It has nothing to do with names or with thinking or feeling. It is not ugly, it is not beautiful, does not owe its shape to volcanic eruption or to erosion by wind, water or ice, has no shape, has no colour, knows nothing of science or aesthetics. Describe it, give it whatever qualities you like, but don't pretend that the description or the qualities have anything to do with the real hill. Don't even pretend that what you see with your eyes has anything to do with the real hill. Because eyesight no less than description is merely human. The hill cannot see. The real hill is something about which you cannot know anything at all.

And in fact this was how the whole landscape began to appear to the tutor – as something dead and boring, not worth thinking about or looking at. Stokes, driving downhill, did not allow the car to increase its pace. He rarely drove at more than thirty-five miles per hour, perhaps in mock deference to Mr Parkin's dignity. Farmhouses, barns, brick-kilns, a pond, a heron, crows, gulls, plough furrows, earthworms, dogs, a woman in an apron. Did it matter which you called which? All names were interchangeable. Any description, any explanation, was as futile as another. Think of all the moods, attitudes, opinions, theories, which the tutor had gone through in a single morning. Which had been right? None. There was no such thing as being right. There were only mental and emotional exercises, some of them prettier than others, and at present they all seemed equally spiritless and flatulent. What was MacCreath talking about at the back of the car?

'They say that the depredations always occur after cubbing.'

His tone was ponderous, careful, as though he were afraid of exciting Mr Parkin by some accidental reference to the races. Mr Parkin said:

'When I was living in Ireland the farmers boycotted foxhunting, and after a couple of years they were down on their knees to us, down on their knees. They put crow's feet in the hedges – you know what – boards with nails sticking out of them. Caw – no use. They were down on their knees to us.'

That was what MacCreath and Parkin seemed to be saying. Seemed. But were they really saying that? Hearing, no less than seeing, was only an exercise, a decoration. The tutor might just as well have heard them saying:

'There's going to be trouble at the races this afternoon.'

'Lucky I brought my six-shooter.'

Perhaps that's what he did hear them saying. It wasn't important. Hearing was something that happened inside your head, not outside it. All sounds were interchangeable and any one sound was as good or as bad as another. Take your choice, invent whatever sounds you like. Don't say – 'The breath force, rising through the glottis, strikes the vocal chords and makes them vibrate'. That is only an explanation, a theory; it tells you nothing about the real human voice. You would have to *be* a human voice before you could know what a human voice really was. And this is everlastingly impossible. The real human voice is unknowable: it belongs to the same unknowable world as beech hedges, farms, crows, hills. The unknowable blurred world slips past the windows of the car. It is eternally heartless, mindless, dead. It is dead even though it moves.

How much better to be eternally dead. Not to think or feel that you are sitting in this car, going to the races. To be dead like this car itself, even though it moves. To be dead like Donald's flesh and bones, even though they grow. To be dead like your own unknowable flesh and bones. The tutor must kill thinking and he must really kill feeling, which still lingered on in spite of his first attempt to kill it. Because if he killed thinking and feeling he would automatically destroy the world of his serfdom, the only knowable world, which after all was nothing more than an evil decoration created by thinking and feeling. He believed that he was beginning to succeed. He sat slack as an old sawdust-filled doll beside the rigid idol Stokes. Or didn't he believe that he was succeeding? Was it just another pretence, a faintly interesting affectation of madness? But even if it was an affectation, that very affectation was a sign that he had become mentally abnormal. Yes, he was beginning to succeed. First the blurred landscape went grey, then it stopped moving, then it went white. Voices at the back of the car became thinner and thinner. Feeling persisted for a time, but at last Stokes dwindled from beside him, slowly as though he had been withdrawn by the hand of a thoughtful chess-player. Feeling shrank inwards from the extremities of the tutor's body, left his hands and arms nerveless, his eyes unseeing, his ears deaf. Thinking moved outwards. Thinking moved in widening circles, getting slower and slower, vaguer and vaguer, like the movement in a cup of tea which has been stirred with a spoon. The violent vortex became smooth, the outer circles moved more and more sleepily.

But, for all that, thinking was not dead, would not die. It was shamming dead. And feeling would not die either. Thinking and feeling had disguised themselves, taken on a new form. Far in the core of his consciousness the tutor was aware of them still. He was aware of a burning area of misery somewhere in the centre of his body. The burning became more and more intolerable. He wanted to be sick, to collapse, to be dead. But it was no use wishing to be dead. He could not become dead by mere wishing.

Thinking and feeling would go on happening now in their new form. If they did not stop soon he must burst or go mad. This was what going mad was like: it didn't kill thinking and feeling, it made them far, far worse than ever. He must get back to where he was before this started. He must get back. Make an effort, however difficult. Try to see something, hear something, move an arm and touch something. Try. Try.

It was startlingly easy. His elbow touched Stokes. He was sitting beside Stokes in the car. The narrow road came towards the windscreen, bringing a copse and a signpost. A nightdress on a washing line, seen through trees. Voices came from the back of the car as before. MacCreath was talking about fishing.

'A clean-run fish with sea-lice under its gills.'

The tutor had recovered, become quite normal again. Thinking and feeling had come back as before. After all, the abnormality had probably been a fake, a deliberate experiment. He had tried to kill thinking and feeling and he had found that it was impossible. He had found also that it was dangerous. Experiment or no experiment, for a moment he had been dangerously near to insanity. He wasn't quite normal even now. The ringing in his ear still went on.

But what a relief to be able to see and hear again. The change made him almost happy. He had taken no fatal step, there were no insuperable obstacles. He realized that for the last three months he had not tried to be happy, had preferred to be miserable. Day after day of cloudy, flatulent misery. Thinking and feeling had been poisoned and had in turn poisoned sight and touch and hearing. Thinking and feeling had poisoned the whole world. And thinking and feeling could not be killed. But couldn't they be changed, couldn't they be healed, drained of their poison? If they could then the whole world would be changed. Because the whole world was a world created by human thinking and feeling and seeing and touching and hearing. Whatever was outside that world didn't count, was dead, couldn't even be called 'something'. He believed it would be possible to make that happy change. He even knew now how he would begin to do it. He would begin again on the lines of the new technique. But the new technique hadn't gone far enough, had been a wretched half-measure, almost worse than no measure at all. The new technique would perhaps have half-changed thinking and feeling, but it would not have changed seeing or touching or hearing. It would not have changed the appearance or the manners of Mr Parkin, it would not have changed the shape of the house or enlarged the tutor's bedroom or shortened his hours of work. It would have accepted these so-called conditions and would merely have altered the tutor's attitude towards them, made him pretend to enjoy them. But the change that the tutor was going to bring about now would be immeasurably more far-reaching. He would change his so-called surroundings, he would not only think and feel differently, he would see and touch and hear differently, as he wanted to, happily. Was that fantastic? He could only know after he had tried it. Better try it at once. Make a bold attempt, look at something, listen to something, see and hear what you really want to. Try. Try.

It was almost a success, seemed at first altogether a success. The landscape, seen through the windows of the car, had lengthened and broadened, become a tremendous panorama. It was like an infra-red photograph. The tutor had the impression that he could see at least fifty miles. And not only had details at a great distance become extraordinarily clear but colours also had become far more vivid. Emerald green and earth-red and ink-black and sea-blue. White insulators on telegraph poles and new copper wires gleamed along the coast road. Behind the town rose a wooden brewery tower and farther up the coast double-wheeled pithead gear. A moving coal-conveyor crawled with rattling buckets to the top of a power station. A small lighthouse stood at the end of one of the stone arms of the harbour. Motor-coaches advanced along the coast road, leaving the town. A crowd of walkers extending over the whole visible length of the road, here scattered and there concentrated in groups, moved in the same direction. At the top of a wooded slope, not very distant now, the grandstand of the racecourse was visible. Far out from the coast a motor-driven fishing-boat showed ink-black on the mounting dead-blue sea. In the foreground a small ivied church stood isolated among variously coloured rectilinear fields. The sky was quite cloudless. The racecourse at the top of the wooded slope appeared to be on a kind of tableland. The tutor noticed, to the right of the grandstand, a large marquee. Its sloping canvas roof was very white. Flags were flying from the roof. The lower part of the marquee, which did not receive the full light of the sun, was grey rather than white. But the roof itself was not so dazzling as the tutor had at first supposed. It seemed to grow dimmer as he looked at it. The sun remained as brilliant as before. The shape of the marquee was changing, was becoming less distinct against the sky. Finally, he was aware of two marquees – one large and beflagged and white, the other small and dull and grey. And the large, the original marquee, seemed to be imposed on the small one, like a superimposed photograph. But the large one grew fainter, became a mere bit of whited gauze, hardly visible.

The same process was going on elsewhere. Everywhere the tutor's vision was fading and another vision, less generous, less detailed, was becoming more and more clearly defined beneath the filmy covering of the original one. The long crowd of walkers dwindled to a few isolated groups, the town seemed much smaller, he could only see two motor-coaches, the lighthouse turned out to be pure gauze, without anything behind it. Nevertheless, the gauze remained gauze, did not altogether vanish.

Much the same thing happened to the tutor's experiment with hearing. He wanted to hear differently, and at first he was startled by his success. Every word of the conversation became as distinctly audible as though Mr Parkin and MacCreath had been alternately whispering into his ear. And not only the vocal pitch but also the subject-matter of their talk was new. They were openly discussing the races.

'It wouldn't surprise me if the M.F.H. withdrew Fritillary and Willie Winkle as well,' Mr Parkin said.

'Why on earth –' MacCreath was astonished, then he laughed. 'You don't believe these tragic stories of ruin he's been telling about himself for the last ten days, do you?'

'There must be something in them.'

'Pure grouch and nothing else. He enjoys it. Ever since he came into his father's estate and paid half a million death duty ten years ago. First he was going to give up fox-hunting. Of course, he did nothing of the sort. Then he couldn't afford motoring. So he bought a new Rolls. Then came the miners' strike, and he was going to be forced to sell his estate and close down his stables and take a small flat in London –'

'It would have served them right if he had,' Mr Parkin interrupted hotly. 'It would have served them right if he'd closed down his estate and his mines and his stables and cleared out of the country altogether. That might have taught them something. All these damned spongers. That would have put them in their place. They think they're too good for the Prince of Wales, let alone the Master of Foxhounds. What's more they get away with it. And the idiots in Parliament wonder why the country is going to ruin.'

'We're a long way from ruin yet,' MacCreath said mildly. 'As a matter of fact, the M.F.H. has been doing very well lately. All his talk about giving up racing is just one of his lighter amusements. And even if he weren't doing well he wouldn't be so foolish as to cut off his nose to spite his face.'

That was the conversation which the tutor heard at first. But as he listened it grew fainter and fainter, became a mere ghost-gauze of sound. And beneath the ghost-gauze another conversation, briefer and more indifferent, grew louder and louder. It was about fishing and fox-hunting:

'... Greenwell's Glory, March Brown, a red-tipped spider.'

'... They say that a fox will never kill in his own locality.'

'... Ever seen a weasel after a rabbit? No matter how many of them cross in front of him that's *his* rabbit. Stops and squeals. Always caught in the end. It's a cruel sport, ha, ha.'

This second conversation – like the second, more meagre landscape – showed that the tutor had not yet conquered his old habits of perceiving. He was still seeing and hearing the same sort of things as before. He must conquer the old habits. He knew now that it was possible to conquer them. After all he had been remarkably successful already – he had seen a new landscape and heard new voices. But he had lacked faith. At the back of his mind he had been unable to believe that the new perception was anything more than a fake. Well, suppose it was a fake – wasn't the old perception just as much a fake, a foisting of human consciousness on to a non-human world? What he had to do was to substitute one fake, the more vital, the happier one, for the other, the habitual one. But could this be done by an act of the will, by mere wishing?

He certainly wished hard enough. He looked again through the car window at the marquee on the tree-surrounded tableland. The gauze outline was still there. It was like a white reflexion on the glass of the window, very faint. It was much nearer to him than the other, the grey and smaller marquee. But, as he looked, the larger marquee moved farther away from him, keeping the same size though now seeming outside the glass of the window. It was about half-way between the car and the top of the wooded slope. It was moving, approaching the smaller marquee. And as it moved it grew more distinct, more solid. And at the same time the smaller marquee began to fade. Yes, the smaller marquee was fading, but the tutor could not make it disappear. Behind the brilliance and the flags of the white marquee it showed small and grey, like a dingy tent seen through a luminous transparent screen. And the tutor was aware that he must not for an instant relax his effort to suppress this small grey remnant. If he did the new vision would fade to a bit of gauze. He must go on wishing the old vision away. But for how long would he be able to go on wishing? He would get tired in the end. Wishing was not enough. There would have to be some change greater than any change that could be brought about by his conscious will. The new vision would have to be independent of his will, would have to be there whether he wished the old vision away or not, would have to be there even if he changed his mind and wished the old vision back. How could that happen, how could the new vision become independent? Could it happen, now, at once?

The tableland and the marquee were suddenly removed from his view altogether. The car was descending into a narrow V-shaped valley. Across the valley the road rose in a wide curve along the right-hand side of the buttress-like wooded slope. Steeply rising trees blotted out the tableland and the marquee. The car approached a bridge at the bottom of the valley. A stream slid over flat rocks. At the end of the bridge the beech hedges on either side of the road were taller than any the car had yet passed. A signpost board was just visible above the hedge on the left-hand side of the road. The tutor regarded it simply as a decoration, and he got a shock when he saw a steam-roller coming out from the concealed side road. But Stokes, who had no visions, had already slowed down. He changed gear, preparing to drive on again. He drove on, passing the steam-roller.

The tutor had time to look carefully at the steam-roller. He looked carefully because it reminded him of something. After his shock he saw it at first as something dangerous, but he soon realized that it was not a danger – it was a power. It was simple and bold and powerful, crested in front with a rampant brass unicorn, thumping with its pistons like a thumping heart. The echoing of its roller over the stones was like the hollow sound of skates on ice. It was bold with the gala boldness of engines stared at by children from a nursery window – big traction engines dragging gipsy caravans to a fair, engines with wire guards over their funnels and with funnels protruding through their long decorated roofs, engines with their long roofs supported by gilded pillars and with dynamos in front of their boilers for making lights on roundabouts in the evening. It was bold with a reminiscent boldness. It was bold with the naive boldness of a child who sticks out his stomach and makes piston movements with his arms in imitation of a big locomotive. It was bold, too, with a maturer efficient boldness, with the boldness of its tall austere-looking driver. It was simple with a generous mechanical simplicity, with the simplicity of its whirling governor and of its ponderous flywheel, of its burnished steering-wheel, and of the wheel at the back for lowering and raising its steel road-breaking teeth. It was powerful with the chuffing indifferent power of a train carrying away a boy to a school which he hates and fears but which he knows nothing can save him from. It was powerful with the sun-glittering power of a motor-coach in which a middle-class young man sets out for an unfrequented part of the country where he thinks he is going to lead the just life, like Socrates. It was powerful with a steaming, sighing power, a power not of despair but of compassion and understanding, as though someone were saying gently to the tutor: 'Remember your past. Look how you have betrayed yourself, wasted yourself, you poor blunderer. How you have brought disaster upon yourself, trying to go your own way. But from now on you will go my way, will be iron, will be new.' It was powerful, more powerful, far, far more powerful with the power of a great mountain which no apathy, no forgetfulness, no wishing can ever destroy. It was the victory of the new vision. Its boldness, its simplicity, its power were what the tutor had wanted to see, had struggled to see, and now they were here before him, outside him, wholly independent of his wanting and struggling. Now he could cease to want and to struggle and the steam-roller would still be there, animating him from outside with its boldness and simplicity and power. The new vision was here and it was solid and real and it could not fade. It was here, it was everywhere. He hardly needed to look elsewhere to prove its ubiquity. He was certain of it. His eyes were full of tears. He had triumphed.

He looked up and saw, only just rising above the trees, the sloping roof of the white marquee. Yes, it was there, real, not gauze. The car was ascending the long curved road up the side of the wooded slope. The steam-roller was already some way behind, at the bottom of the hill. The car was going more slowly. Not only because of the steepness of the hill, but also because of the people who had begun to cross the road. They were evidently taking a short cut to the racecourse. They clambered up the slope to reach the road, crossed the road, slowly climbed the final slope among trees to reach the tableland. Some were shouting, some were chewing stalks of grass, some were smoking, one carried a rucksack, one wore a dirty white sweater and canvas shoes, one a neat blue serge suit, one had the face of a hero, one had a watch-chain hanging from the lapel of his sports coat, one was exuberant, one carried on his shoulder a child waving a cheap Union Jack, one had a flattened syphilitic nose, one played a mouth-organ, one was strikingly good-looking, one had a camera, two were arm in arm, three were playing catch with a rubber ball, all were on the move. They were crossing the road at intervals along a stretch of about a hundred yards. It was like a migration or the storming of a fort. And even when the car had got past this cross-current of walkers, Stokes was unable to drive any faster. The obstruction now was a motor-coach, the last of three that could be seen ascending the road ahead. There was a gilt inscription across its bulging rearside – *Sunrise Coaches*. Its passengers, who were mostly women, were sitting bolt upright and singing. One of them suddenly turned round and leant over the folded hood at the back. She looked at the car attentively, then waved to Stokes with mock coquetry. She quickly turned round again, bursting out into a strong, rather hostile laugh. The coach was all gaiety. People were holding up sticks with brightly coloured pieces of material, flapping like flags, tied on to them. The tutor noticed that the pieces of material were really various kinds of underclothing – drawers, brassières, garters, even corsets. No one in the car except the tutor seemed to be at all amused. Stokes was gloomy, the boy leaned over the tutor's shoulder and stared, and Mr Parkin and MacCreath were talking in very serious tones.

'I didn't like it,' Mr Parkin said.

'Well, whether it was deliberate or not he hasn't done any damage to the car.'

'Imagined he was at the races, perhaps, sir.'

'There you are,' Mr Parkin said to MacCreath. 'He was driving all out round the corner, and he deliberately tried to cut across in front of us. No doubt he'd have liked to send us into the ditch. I've a good mind to inform the police as soon as we arrive at the racecourse.'

'That would make us rather ridiculous,' MacCreath laughed.

'Not ridiculous in the least. Did you notice the fellow's face? Looked as though nothing would have pleased him better than to smash into us. The insolent mucky rat. And he'd have done it, too, if Stokes hadn't slowed down.'

'We can hardly give him in charge for having an unpleasant face.'

'Sneering like a rat looking out of a garbage bin,' Mr Parkin went on pigheadedly. 'Envy and spite are what's at the back of it, the same as with that mob crossing the road just now. If I'd been Stokes I'd have been tempted to run the lot of them down. What the devil are they all doing away from their work in the middle of the morning, anyhow?'

'It's almost one o'clock,' MacCreath said, 'and personally

I must say I'm glad to see so many of them up here at the races. Much healthier for them than getting into mischief in the town.'

'Tcha, it makes me sick. All these rats. Nothing's good enough for them nowadays. Muck, that's what they are.'

Mr Parkin's voice stumbled into silence, finding no adequate words. He was less angry, the tutor thought, than alarmed. The rounded world of his self-importance, more fantastic than any caricature could make it, yet substantial and unique within the bounds of his own household, had collided unpleasantly with a larger world outside. The tutor had found an ally. Mr Parkin was no longer formidable, could even be excused. His frank venom was far less offensive than MacCreath's smug reasonableness.

The car, moving slowly behind the motor-coaches, had almost reached the top of the wooden slope. The white marquee was still there, rising more fully above the trees.

2

The white marquee was here. The car followed the motor-coaches and several other cars into the parking enclosure. A section of the racecourse intervened between the tutor and the marquee. Hundreds of yards of wooden railing, bookmakers' blackboards and giant striped umbrellas, caravans, feet and faces perpetually shifting, gipsies, race-card vendors, miners and office workers, women in hiking shorts and women in expensive toilettes, middle-class young men in tweeds and sleek rentiers in grey top hats, crowds interpenetrating crowds. Single and tall the marquee was here. It was here and it was white and triangular flags flew from its roof and there was nothing visionary about it. It might still seem to have a certain transparency, but that was due to a natural cause – the warm glow of sunlight on an interior canvas wall visible through the turned-back flaps of the entrance. It might seem to have porthole-shaped dormer windows, but that effect was accounted for by the ventilator flaps on its sloping can-vas roof. It might look like an airship: that was because of its rounded ends, its whiteness and its lightness. It might remind the tutor of an aviary: that was explained by the birds flying round it and by the resemblance to thin wires which the guy ropes had when seen from a distance. It might remind him of the sea: the canvas billowing like sails in a slight breeze explained that. It might suggest gardens: there were ferns and vases of flowers on a table just inside the entrance. It might give an impression of leisure and well-being and abundance and freedom: the entrance gave a glimpse of groups of people chatting in easy postures, the interior was filled with cool brightness, the knobs outside which topped the invisible supporting poles were gilded. There was nothing startling about the marquee. It had none of the intensely exciting, apocalyptic quality of the steam-roller. It did not make the tutor feel that some tremendous, almost terrible revolution was taking place in the darkness of his soul. He felt calm and normal. The marquee, in spite of its variety and its bigness, was more ordinary than the steam-roller. He was no longer ecstatic or in tears. He was normally happy. The only abnormality – and this didn't bother him much now – was the ringing in his ear, which was still rather loud.

Luckily this ringing became much fainter as soon as he escaped from the car. It probably had some connection with Mr Parkin or MacCreath or the boy or Stokes, was perhaps a kind of nervous protest against their presence. At any rate, it grew less and less audible the farther he walked away from the car. He was lucky to have escaped from the car as easily as he had. He had stepped out of it at the same moment that Mr Parkin had opened the door at the back, but Mr Parkin had suddenly seen someone in the crowd that he wanted to avoid. The tutor hadn't been sure which of the figures in the crowd Mr Parkin wanted to avoid, but had thought it had been the tall young man with a girlish complexion who had stood beside a small two-seater talking to the car-park attendant.

'There's that young Heseltine again,' Mr Parkin said.

The tutor hadn't heard very clearly the mild question which MacCreath had asked after this, but he had heard Mr Parkin's vigorous reply:

'He's as much right to be a curate at St Saviour's as I have to order a gin and Italian in Buckingham Palace. I don't care to meddle with religion as a rule – I've got no use for it – but I do know there are limits. I've only seen him officiate once and by God I could have strangled him – crossing himself, scratching with his foot like a cock, bowing before he lit the candles, and all manner of vagaries you'd have to see to believe. I could have strangled him with my own hands.'

'And yet,' the tutor thought, walking quickly away from the car, 'if I had suggested that Donald should stop going to church, even for a single Sunday, the old swine would want to strangle me.'

The thought did not make the tutor indignant. He was too interested in getting away from the car. He wanted to be out of sight as quickly as he could, to put as many people between himself and the car as possible. Dodging among the crowd he felt slightly exhilarated, almost wanted to giggle. His escape became easier and easier. It was as though he were running down complicated alleys in a town, continually putting new corners, houses, obstructions, between himself and his pursuers. If Mr Parkin and MacCreath were following him they must almost certainly be thrown off the scent already.

Soon he would be out of danger altogether, an innocent walker in the open country. He was in the open country now. The crowd around him had thinned to a few strollers and the car-park was well behind him. In front of him, about five hundred yards off, was the tall white marquee. But in area at least the marquee was quite dwarfed by the far larger crowd of racegoers. Above their heads it was no more formidable than a half-inflated toy balloon. And the crowd itself was in turn dwarfed by the extremely long racecourse, the distant end of which was dotted with not more than two or three solitary people. And the race-course too was dwarfed, was completely dwarfed by the panorama visible from the tableland – by the variously coloured rectilinear fields, the ivied church, the corrugated farm buildings, the mining town, the power house, the stone-armed harbour, the coast road, the dead-blue sea. And the sky was so penetrated with brilliance that it seemed to have absorbed most of the small molten sun. Brilliance hung in the blue air like millions of evenly distributed diamond particles. The tutor had never felt more serene.

In the equable morning, alone among so many unhurried people, he felt as though he had just woken up on the first day of a long-deserved holiday. He was absolutely calm. What did it matter that the ringing in his ear, very faint indeed now, was still going on? Perhaps it was a good thing that the ringing did go on. Perhaps this acted as a stimulant, preventing him from becoming too much at ease in his new serenity, reminding him of the stingy self-loving life he had so happily escaped from, the three-months' life of petty miseries, comforts, spites, apathies, heroics, smudged vision, woolly hearing, hours telescoping into hours. Or perhaps the far-away mosquito voice was tempting him, saying plausibly: 'Yes, that life had its unpleasant features, but it had pleasant features too. It was a mixture, as all life in this world of ours must be. It was thoroughly human – but is your present mood quite human? Isn't it rather strained and saintly? Will it last, do you think?' The tutor easily repulsed this suggestion. He was absolutely confident that the new serenity would last. It would last for ever. For ever and ever. Or was this absolute confidence of his rather dangerous?

The idea of danger didn't occur to him by chance or as a mere link in the chain of his thinking. The idea had an external cause. For a moment the tutor didn't realize what the cause was, but then he remembered the expression on the face of one of the racegoers whom he had just passed. A very big man, who had been wearing a bowler hat and a dark blue belted raincoat. The expression on his face was difficult to remember clearly, because it had been an unusually complex expression. Not just an ordinary poisonous, vicious, threatening look – it had been far more than that. It had been suspicious and at the same time tumescent with contempt, blackly menacing and at the same time designed to be impressive rather than to threaten an injury. And though quite uncalled for, it had had none of the conscious insolence of the look of a man who takes a dislike to a stranger's clothes or manner: it had been authoritative, firm, profoundly sure of its own rightness – as though this man had caught the tutor committing some elementary offence against common decency. What had the tutor done to evoke it? He felt he must turn round and see it again and make certain that he hadn't been mistaken. Walking very slowly he turned his head. The man still had the same venomous look and was still staring at him. He was a broad, rather fat-shouldered man with prominent ears and with conspicuously large hands. He scraped on the ground with one of his feet, like a fat-shouldered bull which is going to charge. But he didn't move towards the tutor: his object seemed to be solely to make an unpleasant impression on him, to inject a feeling of uneasiness into him. The tutor thought that he might be a detective. He had flat feet and his gross hands were big enough to push down a door or suffocate someone. The tutor turned quickly round and walked on. He certainly did feel uneasy – not so much because of the man's loutish hostility as because he half suspected that the man might have some justification for staring like that. Perhaps the tutor was behaving strangely. What cowardly rot! Had a police spy any right to pass judgement on his behaviour? Of course, his serenity, his private smile, the skip in his walk, his obvious pleasure in his surroundings, would seem strange to a dullard like that. Only dullness, lack of zest, model behaviour, would be understandable to a dullard. Yet think what a weight of legality, what centuries of stupidity such a dullard had behind him. Think how hopeless the position of the solitary must be against him. Men like that have done to death the best spirits in all the ages. And this made the tutor so passionately angry that he immediately stopped walking and turned round to outstare the detective. The same poisonous face as before looked back at him. The tutor might have persisted in his stare, but something distracted his attention. Behind the detective another man, with a face startlingly different from the detective's, was approaching. Lively and pleased, the new face glanced to left and to right, liked everything it saw, finally looked with approval even at the detective, who was still glaring at the tutor. It might have been smelling a rosebush. It was the face of MacCreath.

Jauntily, perkily, walking rather quickly, MacCreath passed the detective and came directly towards the tutor. He did not look at the tutor yet. Very interested he peered aside at the chalked up names and figures on a bookmaker's blackboard, seemed on the point of changing the course of his walk. Delighted, he inclined to the left, saluted an acquaintance, then inclined to the right and resumed his advance towards the tutor. At last he looked at him, dared to give him a restrained smile of recognition. Evidently he had been on the tutor's track for some time, had perhaps followed him all the way from the car. With a certain meekness, as though he was conscious of doing himself an honour, still smiling, he came up to him. For a moment MacCreath's sandy-coloured very short eyelashes were shyly lowered, then he said a little too heartily:

'So this is where you've absconded to.'

'Yes.'

'I came away soon after you did. I remembered I'd promised to go and find my daughters.'

There was nothing in MacCreath's smile to suggest that he had noticed the detective's behaviour. His friendly voice gave no hint of complicity. Nor did he seem to be aware of what the detective was doing now, though without moving his head he could easily have seen him. It was true that the man was no longer blatantly staring at the tutor. He had turned away and was standing with his back towards MacCreath. The thick-fleshed reddish nape of his neck bulged above his coat collar. His hands were behind his back and the thumb of one hand fidgeted between the thumb and forefinger of the other. His face in semi-profile appeared to be watching a bookmaker, but the tutor felt that his interest was really elsewhere.

'Well, what's your fancy for the two-thirty?' MacCreath asked. 'Or don't you go in for that sort of thing?'

The tutor didn't answer, but MacCreath was not at all abashed. On the contary he seemed to be recovering from the shyness he had at first shown. Lively and pleased he once again looked around him, sniffed the eager air of the races. At the same time the detective turned a full profile towards them and squinted at the tutor out of the corner of his eye. Either MacCreath was stupidly, idiotically unobservant or else he deliberately refused to see what was happening.

'I dare say you are not sorry to be relieved of your pupil for a while.'

A sympathetic note had crept into MacCreath's voice. His understanding face, softly ruddy and unevenly discoloured by confused surface ruptures of slight blue veins, looked directly at the detective. Its expression did not change.

'That household must be rather a trial at times.'

He could see, did see. Had seen from the beginning, had fully approved. Thought no doubt that the tutor was making an exhibition of himself. Had come to control him, to soothe him with smarmy pretended friendliness.

The detective turned his head for a moment and faced the tutor fully. His expression was no longer threatening but frigid and boorishly superior. It seemed to say: 'The incident is closed; no need to explain your conduct now.' The tutor was in respectable company and could be let off with a warning. He was in the company of a well-to-do ally of the detective, a disguised ally who used greasier, hypocritical methods. Irritably he broke through MacCreath's friendliness, asked:

'Can't you see that man?'

'Which man?'

'That man. Wearing a bowler. The man you were looking at. You passed right in front of him just now.'

MacCreath was puzzled, but he did not immediately attempt to follow the direction of the tutor's stare. When he did follow it he pretended not to be looking for anyone in particular. He saw the detective, then glanced elsewhere. He waited for some seconds before speaking.

'I don't remember him.'

'He's a detective, isn't he?'

MacCreath gave a respectful little laugh, became aware of the tutor's frown, said diplomatically:

'Is he? How does one detect a detective?'

'There wasn't much doubt about it just now. He might have been going to arrest me.'

'What?'

'I said he might have been going to arrest me. He was extraordinarily offensive.'

The shadow of an amazed suspicion, of a respectable alarm, momentarily clouded MacCreath's good humour. It was as though he were about to ask theatrically: 'Why, what have you done?' Almost at once he recovered himself, said:

'But it's ridiculous. What possible reason could he have for wanting to arrest you?'

'None. I suppose I didn't look rich and seemed to be enjoying myself.'

MacCreath laughed, uncomprehending.

'He can't have meant to be offensive to you. Probably what you saw was just his normal expression – for professional purposes.'

'He did mean to be offensive.'

'But what makes you think he's a detective?'

'His offensiveness.' The tutor, aware of MacCreath's confident incredulity, went on angrily: 'A police spy isn't bound always to be in the right. As a matter of fact he's bound to be in the wrong. A man like that gets to think he can make his own narrow-minded stupidity into a law for everyone else. He thinks he is above the ordinary law. But actually there's nothing to choose between his methods and the methods of so-called criminals. He is a criminal.'

MacCreath laid a gentle hand on the tutor's arm, made him execute an about turn, soothingly urged him into a walk.

'I see what you mean.'

He didn't see, refused to see. The tutor jabbed at him:

'He is the worst type of criminal. Far worse than mere pickpockets or housebreakers. They are only trying to get back what's due to them. They've been cheated out of a decent life, made to live in filthy conditions. He helps to maintain the swindle by criminal force.'

MacCreath said nothing. They were walking towards the marquee. The tutor looked at it with disgust. Its billowing luxuriousness seemed vulgar, flatulently ostentatious. Beyond it and in front of it crowds of people moved towards and alongside the white wooden railing which marked out the course. He no longer saw their diversity, only their dreary cheated sameness. All preoccupied with the thought of the races, swindled by a corrupt circus. MacCreath's face was benignant. He had the admiring look of a worldly-wise grandmother who has been listening to the extravagant talk of a brilliant grandson. But evidently he found the tutor's remarks sufficiently plausible to require a mild rebuff:

'What you say about conditions.... They are very much better now than they were before the war. I know, because I've seen the change in this part of the country with my own eyes.'

MacCreath slid his arm beneath the tutor's. His expensive oatmeal coloured sleeve showed up against the tutor's dingy black overcoat. He had deliberately refused to see the detective's offensiveness. He had refused because if he had allowed himself to see it he would have been forced either to condone it or to condemn it. And if he had condemned it he would have

47

condemned himself. After all, the tutor thought, the detective was really no more than a servant acting in the interests of the well-to-do, subtler, gentlemanly twisters like MacCreath.

The tutor said aloud:

'I was exaggerating when I said the detective was the worst type of criminal. He's only a hired subordinate. I don't suppose he's very highly paid, either.' The tutor tried to disengage his arm from MacCreath's. Controlling his hatred he went on: 'The real criminals are his employers. People who get rich by cheating millions of others out of their right to a decent life. Who are all honey and bogus culture. Profess to believe that the working class they've swindled is very well off. And when anyone retaliates he is arrested and they loftily pretend not to notice.'

MacCreath allowed his arm to fall away from the tutor's. A little less crudely the tutor added:

'People like the M.F.H.'

'But the M.F.H. is about the most harmless and unassuming man I know. He's the last person one would suspect of being mixed up in high finance or anything of that sort. He'd be perfectly content to spend the rest of his life hunting and shooting and racing.'

MacCreath was more startled than hurt by the tutor's attack.

'Besides, he hasn't the business ability to swindle a child.'

'That's just the point,' the tutor said. 'He's got no ability, and yet he's a millionaire. The fact that he isn't capable of doing his own thieving makes him even less excusable. He poses as an amiable country gentleman, and lets his paid agents do the dirty work of collecting his rents and squeezing profits out of his mines.'

Once again MacCreath slid his arm beneath the tutor's. But this time the movement was less comfortable, more hesitant.

'Surely someone must provide the money to keep industry going and to give employment.'

'The M.F.H. provides nothing. His father stole a fortune from the miners and now his agents are using the money as a means of stealing another fortune from them. The only people who really provide anything are the miners themselves.'

MacCreath's arm was quite nerveless, might have been made

of cork. His friendliness had lost all its earlier exuberance. At the same time the tutor, as though new blood had been transfused from MacCreath into him, felt invigorated. His hostility was tinged with pleasure. Even MacCreath's walk had become listless. However, this might not have been due to the tutor. They had arrived in front of the marquee and they were approaching its entrance. Perhaps MacCreath wanted to go in. 'Let him,' the tutor thought. Without decreasing his pace he walked on. MacCreath kept up with him. They had passed the entrance. The tutor had very briefly, contemptuously glanced into the interior of the marquee. But the impression that remained with him after they had passed could not be treated with contempt. When he tried to remember in detail what he had seen he could remember almost nothing except his general feeling that the interior of the marquee was very luxurious. But when he dwelt on this feeling, allowed it to develop in him, certain details emerged from it. A mounted buffalo head jutting from high up on the canvas wall, with a thin rope of dark blue chenille hanging from its horns. A tall panel of glass engraved at its corners with big frosted monograms. On a green baize tablecloth a soda siphon encased in silver tracery. Turkey carpets on the grass. Palms planted in brass-bound mahogany barrels. Cutlery on white table surfaces and above the tables pink and white faces like the faces of waxworks. Flowers seen through the glass of decanters, deceptive as orchids in a conjuror's stage greenhouse. Veering of tobacco breath in subdued sunlight. A black statue of a big-breasted Nubian carrying a basket of gilded pomegranates on her head. Trying to focus these things in his memory the tutor finally lost sight of them altogether. But the impression of luxury remained. The very incongruity of this luxury – whatever its real nature in detail might be – the fact that it had its basis not in some super hotel or clubhouse, but in a marquee on the racecourse, served to intensify his impression. And his disgust at the luxury was tempered by a certain regret, a half-ashamed desire.

MacCreath was speaking again:

'It's a good thing to have ideals.'

The tutor roused himself.

'Who has ideals?'

'To be young and to be without them is not to be young at all. Mind you, I'm not sneering at ideals. I do honestly admire you for them.'

'I loathe ideals. They're a smoke screen for hypocrites. We are told that an ideal can never be realized in practice. Its genuineness can never be tested by mere material standards. Bishops who get their income from armament shares and from slum property are usually idealists.'

MacCreath didn't understand what the tutor meant, but he was discouraged by the tone of his voice. Almost plaintively he said:

'You know you are rather a mystery man.'

'Why?'

'Well, because you are. And the biggest mystery of all to me is how you came to take that job with the Parkins.'

'There was nothing else to take.'

MacCreath was incredulous, ignored the explanation.

'When I heard that they'd engaged a tutor I expected to find someone quite different. Someone of the huntin' and shootin' type, not very strong on the intellectual side. My curiosity was distinctly aroused when I met you.' He hesitated for some seconds before he added:

'I've often wanted to have a talk with you.'

Then, as though he knew in advance that the tutor's reply would be unfavourable, he said despondently:

'I could get you a good job tomorrow. You only have to say the word.'

The tutor's first impulse was to answer with an insult. But something checked him. He stared sideways at MacCreath's face. Beneath its tilted trilby hat it had an air of disillusioned jauntiness, of puzzled desolation. To have answered MacCreath with an insult would have been like injuring an uncomprehending animal. Instead the tutor asked:

'Why do you want to get me a job?'

'I suppose I feel it's your due. You ought not to be allowed to throw yourself away.' MacCreath's voice was embarrassed. 'With your ideas – I call them that because you don't like the word ideals – you ought to be doing something better than private

50

tutoring. You ought to be in a position to mix with really interesting people.'

Interesting people. In other words moneyed people. Twisters. With elegant voices. With delightfully easy manners. Dressed casually or carefully but always in harmony with the occasion. Posed idly in the sunlight on the steps of hotels. Speeding in sports cars. Photographed by flashlight at hunt balls. Talking fashionably and indifferently about art. Owning aeroplanes. Buying themselves on to the stage. Saying a few words at the launching of a submarine. Presented at Court. Playing roulette for charity. Wearing bishop's gaiters and delivering an oily oration in memory of a titled murderer of Indian tribesmen. All that such people said and thought and were and did owed its existence to the poverty and suffering of the working class. Without the workers to feed and house and fetch and carry for them these people wouldn't have time to be so charming. And were they so charming? He became aware that while he had been thinking he also had been speaking. He had felt so angry that he hadn't clearly realized it before. How much he had said aloud he didn't know.

MacCreath had stopped walking. The tutor, mechanically, stopped walking too, heard him say:

'I ought to go back and look for my daughters. I expect they are waiting for me in the marquee.'

The prospect of getting rid of MacCreath may have made the tutor look a little more friendly. MacCreath added:

'Why not come along, too?' Seeing the change in the tutor's look he corrected himself: 'Or perhaps you would rather come along later – after you've had a stroll round the course. The girls would like to see you. Especially Ann.' He was shyly sly: 'You seem to have made a conquest there. She's become quite a socialist since she's known you.'

The tutor could afford to say with perfunctory grace:

'I expect I'll come along.'

He wouldn't.

'I hope you'll think over what I suggested just now,' MacCreath said. 'I should be glad of the chance to do something for you.'

He turned and walked away.

His parting look had been strange, full of pathos. It had been injured and at the same time forgiving. Gently appealing yet infinitely hopeless. He had seemed on the verge of tears. This behaviour hardly accorded with the offer he had made to the tutor a few minutes before. The offer of a corrupt job. A job which would lift the tutor into the ranks of the hypocrites and twisters, the starvers and the murderers. The tutor would never stain his hands with that vileness. Urged by his hatred he began to walk. To walk where? In a negative direction, well away from MacCreath and the marquee. He was carried vigorously forward by the movement of his hatred. But quite soon he came to feel that the vigour was leaking out of the movement. He was walking more slowly. He began to look about him. Other walkers passed by him, receded from him, approached him. A white wooden railing formed a broad semicircular curve to the right of him. Big striped umbrellas rose at intervals in front of the railing. To the left five or six policemen stood in a group, affably chatting, their black chinstraps wagging. He vaguely read the horse names on a bookmaker's blackboard. Fritillary; Willie Winkle; Shalimar; Ichneumon; Furbisher; Easter Egg; Pantechnicon; Waterhole; Bagshaw; The Gaffer. His lapsing hatred could find no point of support in what he saw around him. The racecourse was ordinary and complex, and it was alien to what he had been feeling. It contradicted the simplicity of his hatred, intruded coldly upon him, aroused a new feeling – undefined at first but unpleasant and disturbing.

He tried to revive his hatred by thinking of MacCreath. Walking rather more quickly he mumbled to himself again and again: 'That twister.' The incantation did not satisfy him. He pictured MacCreath's face, wanted to see it twisted with hypocrisy and cunning. But the picture, once evoked, could not be so simply interpreted. It took on a life of its own, independent of the tutor's wishes, faced him once more with MacCreath's strange parting look. The look was inescapably sincere. MacCreath in his limited way meant well by the tutor. He might not understand the tutor's ideas, but he genuinely admired him for having ideas. Saw in him perhaps an integrity and an ability such as he himself had possessed as a young man. Wanted him to prosper, not to be frustrated. Had himself been frustrated, had hoped for and been denied a university education. Had made money instead and betrayed his 'ideals'. Believed that by offering the tutor material help he would save him from the necessity of a similar betrayal. Regarded him as an ally, a champion of his own thwarted aspirations. As a descendant. As an unhoped-for heir who would perpetuate all that had been best in himself. Yet knew in his bones that the tutor would never accept his offer. Knew that he was right not to accept it, that the offer was inevitably corrupt. MacCreath's face confessed it. He understood that he could never have an heir, a son. He would be lastingly frustrated. The tutor might be imagining all this, but he could no longer hope to revive his hatred by thinking of MacCreath. His hatred seemed artificial. A puffed-up religious fake designed to hide something he didn't want to see.

There was something connected with the racecourse that he didn't want to see. The crowd he was walking among had become denser. It was true that none of the people round him showed any hostility to him. Nor were they friendly. They were ordinary and indifferent. Normal. That was the unpleasant and disturbing thing. The ordinary racecourse was a part of the ordinary landscape, and the landscape extended to the place he had come from this morning. The house with four lawns. His futile job as a tutor. That was the sordid actuality which his high-falutin hatred had tried to conceal. And that actuality was winning against him, had already begun to make him feel depressed and afraid.

The crowd was becoming much denser. He could no longer move forward through it. He had arrived at the outer fringe of a close-packed circle of people. They were mostly men, and they were watching something. A clear space in the middle of the circle was occupied by some kind of performer. He was wearing a maroon-coloured silk dressing-gown, and a marmoset was perched on his right shoulder. His face seemed familiar. It was sardonic, pug-nosed and bulging-eyed. It was the face of Stokes, but his hair was the wrong colour. He was not Stokes. He was someone extraordinarily like him. In his left hand he held a green apple. His fingers twirled it, tossed it into the air, caught it. From his busily-working mouth came a continuous patter. His words were not clearly articulated, but the tutor could distinguish now and again, or thought he could distinguish, what the man was saying.

'...Step on the juice, Archibald.... Shakespeare, stratosphere, bottled beer.... You're smiling at my monkey, madam? Poor little fellow.'

He carefully raised his right arm and tickled the marmoset with the tip of his finger. The animal turned and pressed its face into his ear. Its almost transparent tail hung down over his brilliant silk shoulder. All the time he was twirling and tossing the apple with his left hand.

'That's a secret between us that was. Archie was telling me what a fine lot of folks he could see hanging around. All the best people are heeah today. You're here, I'm here. We're all heeah. ...Bogey, Bogey.... Have you seen the girl with the dreamy eyes?...'

The tutor was still on the fringe of the crowd, but the man's voice was becoming more distinct.

'Couldn't get along without my Archibald. Fetches my breakfast for me every morning. First met him out in South America. An old sailor sold him to me for luck. Banana bugs they call 'em out there. It's a grand country. All the flowers and the birds, grand birds. Pick and choose. With her ding-dongs dangling in the dust. You needn't look at me like that – I didn't say nothink. Hoojabifiblia.'

The man's lips curiously failed to synchronize with the sound of his words. He was like a talking-film that had gone slightly wrong, the tutor thought.

'Yes, I've seen a bit of the world in my day. And, touch wood' – he touched his head – 'I'll live to see some more. Had my ups and downs. You mightn't think I'd been at Oxford University with the Prince of Wales. It's a fact. At Worcester College he was. Under the same roof. Now I'm here. Horses, geegees – that's my trouble. Don't think I'm blaming my luck. Do you know why I've got you folks together here today? Because my luck's going to change, and I want you to share it with me. In another minute I'm going to give you the winner of the big race. Luck doesn't run one way for ever and mine's just about to turn. Trust to luck and never say die. There's nothing else you can trust. I'm not being irreverent. All of us heeah know the etymolological derivation of the word 'clergy'. It comes from an old Greek word meaning 'to gamble'. You see, the first parsons were all chosen by lot, because luck is really the will of the Almighty, and there was no better way of finding out which ones He didn't want. Gambling is the ruling passion of mankind and the Lord God Himself put it in us. All over the world you'll find it – in Asia, in New Zealand and the Fiji Islands. Every single human being is a gambler, not only the lazy good-for-nothing fellows. Who could work harder than a Chinaman? Yet in his leisure moments John will think nothing of hazarding a week's wages on such games as fan-tan, pak-a-pu, and chuk luk.'

He paused to take a bite out of the green apple.

'Hullo,' he said with mock surprise. 'Something's been at this before me. The strangest apple I ever.... Will some lady or gentleman be kind enough to lend me a silver fruit knife?'

The audience laughed. He dexterously spun the apple between the first fingers of his two hands. The part of it he had bitten formed a rotating band of white. The marmoset was shivering.

'I believe we are on the threshold of a secret. I have a feeling that at any moment now we may be told something important. Something all of us are itching to know.'

A little hunchback, very obviously an accomplice, stepped out of the crowd and handed him what looked like a large hunting knife.

'Thank you sir. Just what I wanted.'

He began to peel the apple.

'Who can tell me the winner of the two-thirty? I can, said the sour old fruit.'

He dug the point of the knife into the apple, pretended suddenly to notice a face in the crowd.

'Oh, no, sir, not you, sir. This old fruit in my hand I meant.'

He split the apple into halves.

'Me-he, me-hi, me-soomp-soomp-soomper-diddle, whip bang periwinkle, nip-coom, ni-caht.... Hullo, what's this?'

55

He delicately drew out a small piece of folded paper from the core of the apple.

'A love letter from a maggot. What wouldn't you give to hear me read it?'

The crowd began to throw coppers towards him. He smiled his thanks, but did not try to catch the coppers, nor was he in any hurry to pick them up off the ground. He fingered the folded paper:

'It's getting hot.... *Shakes*peare *strato*sphere, *bott*led beer. ...*Hor*ses, *gee*gees, thoroughbred, gingerbreads, screwlegs, bandylegs, spindlelegs, featherbeds.... Bogey, Bogey, Archibald.... And the lucky winner...Is...Is...Have you seen the girl with the dreamy eyes? Is, is, is, is, IS...'

He unfolded the paper.

'Easter Egg.'

He glanced impressively round at the crowd.

'At fifteen to one, boys. A real gold mine.'

He suddenly saw the tutor. His expression changed. Perhaps the tutor, without knowing it, had looked sceptical and superior. The man was vigorously angry, shouted:

'Break into your cash box, you bounder.'

No one in the crowd turned to look at the tutor.

'Show your face, you maggot. You can't hide from me. I can see you trying to cringe behind the ladies' backs. And well you may, you...'

The tutor was horribly embarrassed, but the crowd showed no sign of interest in what the man was saying.

'I know you. I know your type. I've got you taped all right.'

As before, the sound of the man's voice failed to correspond with the movements of his mouth. But there was nothing ambiguous or unconvincing about the words which the tutor heard.

'Yes, you. You with the face of an out-of-work chapel minister. You're the sort that makes good luck turn sour. You'll never gamble. You wouldn't stoop to anything so petty, eh? You care for higher things. If you were offered a thousand pounds tomorrow you wouldn't take it, eh? So you think. Nor you wouldn't either, not if there was any risk attached. I know you and your *principles*, my lad. I could turn you inside out with my little finger. You suppose I haven't ever heard of Socrates? I was studying him before you were born. And I'm not saying that in his day there wasn't a lot of sense in him. What year of grace do you think you're living in, you glum-faced ninny? Don't tell me you don't know? I shouldn't be surprised to find you a couple of months out in your dates. But not as much as one thousand nine hundred and ninety-nine years. I'll tell you straight what I think of your principles. You don't believe in 'em any more than I do. You only pretend to. Because you are in a bad funk. You are as keen to lay your hands on the goods of this world as the worst of us. But you're afraid you might put your fingers round a stinging nettle instead of a five-pound note. So you kid yourself that your principles are finer than gold. In other words, you're a sop, you're a weakling, you're a sissy.'

The man was not even looking at the tutor now. He was bending down and had begun to pick up coins from the grass. The voice went on:

'I'm telling you for your own good. Wake up and be a man. Be human. You're British, aren't you? Then learn to take reasonable risks and don't always be worrying for the safety of your own skin. Know what you want and don't be afraid to go right ahead and get it. All the good things in life can be yours, if only you'll make up your mind to take them. The really good things, I mean, not just the cheap and flashy makeshifts. Don't you want to be in love with a really beautiful woman? Aren't you ashamed when you think of your present condition – without any woman at all? Don't you want to travel, to see the world? Don't you want a home of your own? Don't you want a good job and plenty of friends? Yes, you want all these things. Why be afraid to admit it?'

The man had finished picking up the coppers. As he dropped the last of them into his pocket he said with a wink at the crowd:

'Win it and wear it, like the wooden leg at the battle of Balaclava.'

The show was over. The man's face relaxed, disburdened itself of its artificial animation. He did not walk away, did not even take off his dressing-gown, but the people round him no longer gave him their undivided attention. He had retired into himself, was becoming one of the crowd. In a moment the circle would disintegrate and everyone would walk away. The tutor must speak now. He must get even with this nauseous charlatan. Speak, denounce, vomit out words of boundless disgust. British. Luck. Sissy. Be a man. Spew these words back at him, clotted with bilious loathing. You degenerate, muck-brained, syphilitic, superstitious swine. Then the man would retort violently. Suppose there was a fight and the tutor won, would that prove that he did believe in his principles? Already the crowd was beginning to move away. Or could he say with perfect calm – 'I am not a weakling. I believe in intellectual and emotional integrity. I do not want to be a vulgar success or to make my mark in the material world. I know I am right, and this man's would-be insults mean nothing to me.'? It would be a lie, and the crowd would roar with laughter. The tutor knew he did not believe in his principles. He was not a monk, he did not believe in self-abnegation, he did want to live. Flabby with misery he began to walk away. He did want to live, but not to live like that charlatan, not like the crowd on the racecourse, not like MacCreath or the Parkins. He was afraid that if he tried to live he might become like other people. But other people did try. Even though they had made a mess of their lives they were not cowards. They were better than he was.

They were more than better – they were admirable. These people among whom he was walking had lived through horrible difficulties, had not surrendered. Poverty, ignorance, diseases – his woes were a luxurious fad compared with theirs. Yet most of them looked cheerful. They did not smell out vileness everywhere, as he did. They were not negative, did not draw back in disgust from life. His job with the Parkins would seem a happy sinecure to them. And with very little effort he could get a better job than that. He could accept MacCreath's offer. 'It is not too late,' he thought. He had stopped walking. A few yards in front of him a narrow sandy road cut across his path at right angles, and along this road from the left two cars were approaching. Sunlight glittered on the chromium-plated radiator of the first car. 'Why not accept?' he thought. The joy and the splendour of life. Success. The chance might never come again. The first car, moving slowly, was passing in front of him. It was an open touring car, very big but not big enough for the number of people in it. Yet they did not give the impression of being uncomfortably huddled together. They luxuriated; some reclining, some gracefully leaning, others as easily upright as flowers. They were all young. Only one of the men wore a hat, and none of the girls was fashionably dolled up for the races. All – men and girls – seemed good-looking. One of the men, the tutor thought, was playing a mandolin. A girl was dressed in mauve gauze. Another man was holding a butterfly net. A girl had a large slim book beneath her bare arm. The tutor thought he recognized Humphrey Silcox at the driving wheel. The car had passed. From the dickey of the second car a girl waved to the tutor. She was Ann MacCreath. The second car stopped. Ann called to him:

'Come with us for a drive round the course.'

Dorothy MacCreath, sitting at the wheel, smiled at him. From behind her head the dark red face of a young man peered keenly, with virile friendliness. The tutor ran across the grass and climbed into the dickey.

This car, unlike the first, was not crowded. Before the tutor had arrived only three people had been in it. He wondered whether Ann had intentionally reserved a place for him, had been looking out for him. Dorothy was driving slowly, because of the crowds. The first car was about thirty yards ahead. To the right extended the white wooden railing which marked out the course. The narrow sandy road ran parallel with the course, and in the distance both road and railing curved sharply. The car would eventually arrive back at the marquee, the tutor thought. To the left the tableland ended in an abrupt invisible slope, defined only by the descending tops of a few fir trees. Beyond the slope stretched a huge plain of variegated green. Smooth isolated hills broke up the line of the horizon. The sun was brilliant. Travel, love, joy, creation – nothing would be impossible for the tutor. 'All the worlds of nature and of art,' he said to himself. What wouldn't he do, what sights, odours, feelings he would savour.

Don't wait a moment longer. Oh, begin, begin. But he had already begun. He was saying aloud to Ann:

'Come to Reykjavik.'

She looked at him with sober friendliness, unsurprised, but she did not answer. He went on vehemently:

'Anywhere, Ecuador, London. Now. Just as we are. With no preparations. Without even a toothbrush. Clear of all impedimenta. Nothing. Everything.'

Still she was not startled, did not speak.

'Why not? What's to stop us?'

She grinned pleasantly.

'Say something,' he insisted.

'You don't really mean it.'

'I do. Provided we start at once.'

She laughed.

'The fact is you don't want to come,' he said.

She was slightly annoyed for a moment:

'How could we start at once without any preparations? It just isn't practical.'

'That's the whole point. If it were practical it wouldn't be worth doing. If we had to collect toothbrushes and make all kinds of plans for the journey we might as well stay where we are. We can get as much practicality as we like here and now without travelling for it.'

'But we should have to take *some* kind of practical action. Get out of this car, for instance.'

'No. If both of us really wanted to go we should *find* ourselves out of the car. We shouldn't have to *get* out. We shouldn't have to make a cheap conscious effort of will.'

She was grinning again. He added:

'You wouldn't come even if I did agree to be practical.'

'Yes, I would.'

'I don't somehow see us getting married.'

'Who suggested marriage? Two people can go away together for a few weeks without binding themselves for life. *I* am in no hurry to get married.'

'A few weeks is a long time. We might become more involved with each other than we meant.'

'A few days then.'

'I don't know.'

'Or a single night.'

She was quite serious. But he no longer felt any enthusiasm for her. He looked into her face. It was well-proportioned and healthily coloured. It had no make-up on it. It was soberly intelligent. There was nothing enigmatic or disturbed about it. Perhaps there was a hint of pique in her voice as, realizing his change of feeling, she said:

'How long will you go on allowing the Parkins to decide what you do?'

'Not much longer.'

'You said that before.'

'Yes.' He was mysterious: 'But now I know I can get another job as soon as I want it.'

'What sort of job?'

'A better one.'

'You will find it just the same. Until you begin to act up to your opinions you will find any job the same.'

He wanted to say, 'I have changed my opinions,' but he could not. He became angry:

'I haven't particularly noticed *you* acting up to your opinions. Or perhaps you merely pretended to have the same ideas as I did, from ulterior motives.'

'You know that's rubbish. I didn't agree with you at first, and I didn't pretend to. But I became convinced you were right. And I *have* tried to do something about it.'

'Oh? What? Been manufacturing bombs in the attic?'

'You are just being childish. Anarchists and fascists manufacture bombs. We are opposed to assassination.'

'Well, what exactly have you done?'

'I have been selling pamphlets down at the docks.'

'Have you?'

'Yes. Tomorrow evening I am going to speak in public for the first time. In the street.'

Aware that he might think her boastful or romantic, she added:

'Of course, my main work will be among the middle class. You have to be a docker yourself if you hope to have real influence with dockers. But I want to get experience among the working class first.'

'What sort of experience do you think you are getting up here at the races? Or is this your first attempt to work among the middle class?'

She had a moment of honest awkwardness.

'No, I admit I didn't come here to work.' She recovered her assurance: 'But it won't do. I wouldn't go away with you even if you were practical. I have been deluding myself that I could live with a foot in both worlds. No one can be a socialist half the time and go for romantic pleasure jaunts the other half.'

Unreasonably he felt disappointed. She went on:

'It might be different if you were a socialist. Then there would be no question of our relation becoming a mere pleasure jaunt. The strange thing about you is that you see quite clearly what is wrong with the system under which we are living. More clearly than I do. But you take no action. You are content to hate and despise your life.'

'No.'

'Then what action do you take?'

How could he explain? He couldn't say: 'I have done nothing yet, but I intend to accept a good job which your father has offered me. I intend to be a success.' That would be hopelessly crude, not at all what he really meant. He meant to live a happy and splendid life. He meant to live it at once, to win a whole world of poetry and love. That was the action he would take. Now, in the slowly moving car, with Ann beside him. But her serious face checked him, and she said:

'You think you can get a better job. Perhaps you can. A better-paid job, with fewer petty restrictions on your leisure. You may even have a liberal-minded employer. But unless you fight against capitalism you will feel just as servile as you do now. You will never be free in your mind and heart so long as all your actions, your real life, are still wholly in the service of the rich.'

He recognized phrases which he himself had used in an earlier conversation with her. He did not answer, stared out of the car at the racecourse.

'Or have you changed your mind about capitalism? Perhaps you think now that there is nothing seriously wrong with it and that it has a brilliant future. Or that it doesn't exist.'

Still he would not speak. He looked at the first car, saw the girl in mauve.

'Suppose you get a good job and make money. Suppose you become a capitalist. I can hardly imagine it, but if it did happen do you think you would be able to live the sort of life you want to? Your time would be mostly taken up in trying to squeeze profits out of the workers and in helping your friends to prepare for war. That's what capitalism increasingly leads to – not to a new world of poetry, love and science. You would have no option – unless you were ready to destroy yourself as a capitalist.'

The sandy road, keeping parallel with the white railing, had straightened out after a wide semicircular bend. It extended forward in the direction of the car park, then curved away again to the right. The girl in the first car looked back at him. Ann went on:

'Fascist war has already begun, and it will spread. How far it will spread will depend on how soon the workers' movement can become strong enough to stop it. We need all the allies we can get. We need them now.'

He felt a slight awkwardness, but he refused to argue.

'Why not come down to the docks with me tomorrow?'

He would have to say something soon. He looked at the girl in the first car, at the white railing curving away to the right, at the shifting crowds ahead. He was reassured.

'No,' he said. 'Anyway, not tomorrow.'

It was necessary to take action, but not Ann's sort of action. It was necessary for him to stop indulging in passive fantasies which left his real situation unchanged, but this did not mean that he must at once begin to lead the life of a militant socialist. There was no war here on the racecourse, and the capitalists who had come here had not come in order to prepare for war. Nor were the crowds of workers visibly being sweated or oppressed. Her ideas seemed abstract, irrelevant to the concrete reality which was before his eyes. What he must do was to recognize that reality and try from now on to act in accordance with it.

Ann's voice continued, but he no longer heard what she was saying. As the car curved along the curving road to the right the marquee came into view again. The girl who had returned his look was not, as he had first imagined, dressed in mauve gauze. Nor did one of the men hold a butterfly net, and the large slim book under the bare arm of another girl was also an illusion. These extravagances had been a trick played on him by his excitement. He was normal again now. He would be objective and practical. His view of the marquee was normal, was not influenced in any way by the different kind of excitement which he was now beginning to feel and which he must carefully control. On the contrary his new feeling was due to, was influenced by the objectively real marquee. Just to prove the efficiency of his control he stopped looking at the marquee for a moment, glanced once again at the people in the first car. There was nothing fantastic about them. They were ordinary upper-middle-class young men and women. Most of the men did in fact wear hats, no one was playing a mandolin, and the girl who had looked at him was dressed not in mauve gauze but in a fur coat – though it was true she did wear also a blue silk scarf. The tall man leaning against the side of the car, half sitting on the door, had a pallid puffy face like the face of an unhealthy boy. The tutor's earlier impression that everyone in the group was splendidly beautiful and unconstrained was a sickly make-believe. Yet he would have been equally deceived if he had regarded them as vile twisters smelling of carrion. He must try to see the actuality which was before his eyes. The fur coat might or might not be expensive and fashionable – that was a matter for abstract speculation. But its smoothness, its neat straightness descending from the fur-buttoned waist, its delicate fullness gathered into folds on either side of the open neck – were in *fact* difficult not to admire. The girl might or might not use cold cream or spend hours at the dressing-table – but the sun's warmth glowed in the frosty pendants of her earrings and illuminated the human warmth of her face with a cool bloom as of ice. She looked at him again and he looked away. The tall man was talking to someone. His puffy face was transformed with a new whimsical vigour. Suddenly the tutor understood the truth about these people. They were better, more beautiful, less constrained, more intelligent than most other people. They were not twisters like the charlatan with the apple, nor did they cringe away from life like the tutor. They dared to live in the world, and they lived better, more sanely, more happily than others.

Why shouldn't he become one of them? But he *was* one of them. He was after all not an ugly duckling, not a coward, not a failure. He had seen the swans flying. A wild cry of recognition and of freedom rose in his throat and he wanted to shout to the people in the first car: 'At last I am here.' But he restrained himself. He must be practical and objective. He looked again at the marquee.

His sense of control was becoming in itself an excitement. He felt as though he was in solitary command of some huge unexplored power-house. Or as though he was very ingeniously, with consummate mastery, concealing the fact that he was drunk or mad. But was this control natural? Wasn't it a new form of mysticism, of self-abnegation? Why shouldn't he dare give free play, within sane limits, to a happiness which was based no longer on fantasies but on the actual possibilities of his real surroundings? He relaxed his control. The marquee looked the same as before. Only his feelings had changed, had expanded their power, risen at last to the actuality which was before his eyes. The marquee was not like a racing-yacht in full sail, it was not like a white-walled aerodrome from which he could instantly fly to any part of the world, it was not like a crowded flutter of girls' frocks along the esplanade, was not like a mansion with circular mansard windows and broad white pillars and porticoes and gilded urns, not like a cool place for the protection of art and learning, not like a white balcony from which he could look at mountains through a powerful brass telescope. It was like an ordinary marquee, white and rather large. It was like the actual destination towards which a slowly moving car was taking the tutor. It was like a real place where the people in the first car would soon arrive, where he, too, would arrive, and where he would be able to meet some of them; was like an opportunity for beginning to make friends with them, or at least for striking up an acquaintance with them which later, after he had accepted

65

MacCreath's offer, he would be in a position to develop further; was like a first step towards not an ideally happy future but a life much happier than he had lived in the past, a life in which travel, yacht-racing, flying, views of mountains, art and learning, girls, visits to mansions, would be practical possibilities. The marquee was like the headquarters from which he would begin his practical campaign to get what he knew he wanted.

'Travel,' he thought. Almost at once – or did the event precede the thought? – the car stopped. The first car, which was now only a few yards away and was directly in front of the main entrance of the marquee, had also stopped. The tall man and the girl in the fur coat and all the others except the driver, Humphrey Silcox, had got out. Someone who had not been in the car had come forward out of the shadow of the marquee entrance and was speaking to Silcox. The others turned to look at the newcomer. He wore a dark blue belted raincoat. Without alarm or revulsion the tutor recognized him as the detective.

Ann leant forward to ask Dorothy:

'What's happened?'

'Tod's going to find out.'

Dorothy's red-faced young man had jumped from the car and was striding towards Silcox and the detective. He was broad-backed, stocky and powerful, and his long arms swung heavily from his shoulders. Dorothy and Ann got out of the car. Tod listened for a moment to what the detective was telling Silcox, then said curtly and loudly:

'We'll take them round to the side.'

The detective shook his head. His look was agreeable and regretful, suggested that he knew he was making an absurd demand but that no other course was open to him. Tod turned away from him with contempt, walked back towards the second car.

'What is it?' Dorothy asked.

'We've got to take the car round to the car park.'

'Why?'

'Just darned officiousness.'

The tutor was climbing out of the dickey. Dorothy moved to regain her seat at the driving-wheel, but Tod intercepted her.

'I'll drive it round for you,' he said definitely. 'You go and enjoy yourself in the marquee with the others.'

Without waiting for her assent he stepped into the car. Then, as though he at last felt free to concern himself with something that really interested him, he looked at the tutor, asked confidently:

'You coming?'

His unhesitating grin overpowered the tutor's disinclination.

'Yes.'

In any case the tutor would be able to return to the marquee later. He found himself in the act of sitting down in the front seat of the car. Tod was pushing the gear lever into reverse. The car bounded backwards, curved with a jump from road to grass, struck the canvas wall of the marquee. The brakes squeaked, Tod changed gear, the car moved forward with an accelerating swerve and jerked on to the road again. People were crossing the road, but Tod did not slow down for them.

'There's a type that makes me feel sick,' he said.

'Where?'

'That meddling sod we've just left. I can't think why Silcox wastes time talking to him.'

'The tutor realized with sudden pleasure that Tod was speaking of the detective.

'He reminds me of some of the specimens the government sends out to Nigeria. Just because they are officials, my God, they think they know your business better than you do yourself. It's getting worse every year.'

The tutor began to be glad that he had not stayed behind at the marquee. Here was someone who spoke his language, felt as he did. He asked with admiration:

'What's it like out there?'

'Not so good as it was. Too much government interference. And plenty of damned hard work. Still, I don't mind that. The pay's good enough.'

The tutor was eager to be sympathetic:

'What sort of job do you do?'

'Tin-mining. Not underground, you know – alluvial. I'd stick it for another year or two, but I doubt whether the life out there would suit Dorothy. Climate's the main snag.'

In spite of the speed at which Tod drove, the tutor did not feel there was any risk that he might knock someone down. People stood aside for him, and showed no resentment. And if someone had suddenly stepped out on to the road the tutor knew that Tod would have been able to pull up without the least difficulty. His driving was as controlled yet vigorous as his voice.

'But there are advantages. Besides the pay. I've a large house and servants to do all the odd jobs and a garden very nearly as big as an English estate.'

Ignoring the road for a moment, he turned to the tutor with a grin:

'Guess what breed of watch-dog I keep in my garden.'

'Well, what sorts of dogs are there in Nigeria?'

'It isn't a dog,' Tod almost crowed. 'It's a mandrill. You know – with a crimson and blue bottom. That's a fact. Better than any dog. No risk of burglars – it could fetch 'em down as quick as a tiger.'

His face had turned again to glance ahead. It was big-nosed and heavy-eyebrowed beneath a severe backward sweep of sleek black hair. Normally it would have seemed aggressive, but now its grimness of feature was broken by a look of happy friendliness. Evidently he liked the tutor.

'You're tutoring that Parkin boy aren't you?' he asked.

'Yes.'

'How do you like the job?'

'I don't.'

The tutor had a moment's uneasiness. But Tod, far from thinking him a muff or a grouser, was very pleased.

'There aren't many decent jobs going at home now.' His tone changed: 'Unless you happen to be the son of a company director. Like a fellow I knew at the mining school. No brains, and hadn't the guts of a louse. But he's fallen on his feet in one of the few mining jobs left in Cornwall.'

Tod's anger soon cleared.

'Anyway I've no intention of sticking in Nigeria for the rest of my days. I'm going to take up fruit farming. Down south, near Jo'burg.'

'Where's that?'

mandril

'Johannesburg. Out there we always call it Jo'burg.'

Once again Tod glanced away from the road, looked full at the tutor.

'Why don't you come out too? You could get a good job as lecturer at the university. Decent pay – enough to marry on.'

In an instant the tutor knew what he would do – he would go out to South Africa. Not to stay there permanently, not even to stay there for a whole year, but as a beginning of his travels. He wanted to explain this to Tod, to confide in him and at the same time to use words which would convey not too fulsomely how much he admired him. 'You are the real traveller, the pioneer, the genuine man of action,' he thought. He did not say this, or anything like it. For the moment he said nothing at all. Tod, for the first time since they had left the marquee, was concentrating his whole attention on driving the car. They were arriving at the car park.

The attendant came towards them. Tod steered the car into a narrow gap between two other cars. The engine stopped. He paid the attendant a shilling for a ticket. The attendant walked away. Tod stepped out on to the running-board, suddenly stumbled. Perhaps he fell against the door handle of the adjacent car. The tutor at first saw only the crouching curve of his back, then with a shock noticed his face. Its expression suggested fear rather than pain. It was like the face of a man who knows he has been hit by a poisoned arrow. The tutor hurried towards him round the back of the car.

'Have you hurt yourself?'

'No. I'm all right. Let's get out of here.'

Tod straightened himself. Staring in front of him he began to walk. The tutor kept up with him.

'I don't want to run into Silcox just at present,' Tod said.

With an almost savage effort he increased his pace.

'I couldn't stand his chatter.'

They arrived back at the entrance of the car park. Outside Tod turned to the left, away from the road and on to the grass. He began to walk more easily. There was no sign that Silcox's car had yet started from the marquee.

'I get these attacks now and again.'

'What are they?'

'My malaria. A dose of quinine will put me right.'

Tod was gloomy.

'I can't even play a game of tennis now without wondering all the time whether I'll be in bed for days afterwards.'

He was walking faster again. The tutor asked sympathetically:

'I suppose almost everyone gets it out in Nigeria?'

'Yes. Or something worse. You need a first-class physique if you're to stand up to the life out there even for a couple of months.'

'I can see that.'

The tutor sounded more impressed than he really felt now. Tod was flattered.

'And diseases aren't the only thing you're up against.'

His voice mysteriously stopped.

'What else?' the tutor asked.

'I expect you've wondered whether there's any truth in the stories about Englishmen who go native.'

'Yes.'

'Well, there is. It's more common than you'd think. I had to go and see a fellow on business who had been out there seven years. He was living with a black woman, and when I went to bed I found he'd provided me with one too. That was his idea of hospitality. I kicked her out.'

Tod was beginning to enjoy himself. His attack of malaria couldn't have been very severe.

'And the natives think nothing of offering you their wives. One evening my cook-boy brought me in a couple of black mams. He couldn't understand why I knocked him down.'

The tutor found it more and more difficult to maintain his enthusiasm for Tod. Even travel seemed less attractive now – though not because of the black mams.

'Drink's another thing. If you don't drink the climate gets you down, and if you do you have to know when to stop. You can't afford to be weak-willed. There was an Englishwoman in the lounge of a hotel at Lagos who was so doped that she allowed the Pekinese on her lap to bite away most of her left bub. The rest of it had to be amputated afterwards.'

70

The marquee was about a hundred yards in front of them. Perhaps less, but their route towards it across the grass was not as direct as the road would have been. Miles beyond it and far below it rose the rectilinear fields, the long coast road, the dead-blue sea. Without regret the tutor suddenly gave up the idea of travel, at any rate of Empire travel. Tod went on:

'I wouldn't care to introduce Dorothy to the life out there. Mind you, I'm not questioning her pluck – she'd face up to it all right. But Nigeria's no place for a white woman.'

His malaria seemed to affect him again. He stumbled against the tutor, recovered, said sourly:

'Someone's given her the idea that she won't like Jo'burg.'

His tone at once became milder, almost sad. He confided in the tutor:

'When I first suggested fruit-farming she was very keen about it. Then she changed her mind. Yesterday she told me that she didn't want to leave England. She'll change her mind again, of course. She would never have had any doubts in the first place if it hadn't been for her sister's influence.'

He added with manful tact:

'I'm not saying a word against Ann. She's a fine girl, and I wish you the very best of luck. But I think you ought to know something about the sort of people she's been mixing with lately. If anyone can get her out of their hands you should be able to.'

The tutor looked with relief at the marquee. It was not much more than fifty yards off now.

'I don't know whether you know it, but they are socialists of the worst type. Not just the weak-kneed parlour sort – real scum from the gutter. Most of them Jews.'

Tod's voice had become strangely like Mr Parkin's. It had the same vicious jerkiness, but it was more dangerous, less easy to ignore than Mr Parkin's.

'There's only one thing to do with that sort of muck.'

The tutor tried to concentrate his attention on the marquee. How white it was, and how near. Soon he would be inside it, talking to someone else. But Tod's voice could not be evaded.

'Knock 'em down before they guess what's coming to them. I shot a nigger in Nigeria for far less than some of the things

71

they've done. I had to – or sooner or later he'd have murdered me.'

Tod was deliberately walking more slowly.

'God knows why you people at home have allowed them to get away with it for so long. They've practically smashed the army and navy and left us with the weakest air-force in Europe. And it isn't as though you'd have had any trouble in stopping them.'

The absurdity of his words made his voice sound unreal. It was less like a voice than a nasty sultriness in the air, an apprehensive heaviness closing in upon the tutor.

'Deal with one or two of them and the rest would scuttle like rats. They may be well paid by the Soviet for undermining our defences, but they'd soon drop it if they thought they might get hurt.'

The voice came closer to the tutor's ear.

'Do you know what they did down here at the Election?'

'No,' he said weakly.

'They slashed all the tyres on the M.F.H.'s car. I saw it myself soon afterwards. But the next night we were ready for them. I don't think they'll try that trick again.'

Tod abruptly stopped walking.

'I wonder whether they're up to something today?' he said.

A stimulating idea had occurred to him.

'That fellow who told us to take away the cars may not be such a fool after all. Perhaps he thinks there's going to be trouble. He may need our help. Those scum are always on the look-out for the M.F.H., and they know he'll be up here today.'

The idea was so patently ridiculous that the tutor mechanically received it as a joke.

He tittered, then became conscious that Tod was glaring at him. He tried to justify himself.

'It's hardly likely they'd think of attacking the M.F.H. on the racecourse.'

'They won't get the chance to think. We'll see to that. We'll do all the thinking, and we'll do it first.'

Tod's look was aggressively suspicious.

'I wasn't blind at the Election and I know most of them by sight, and even if I didn't I could spot them from a mile off by their noses.'

His face came nearer to the tutor's, grew bigger. Its red was minutely dotted with points of black, and from its forehead the greased hair went backwards in blackly shining strips. The tutor hadn't the energy to move his own face away from it.

'Hit them before they've got a chance to hit you – that's the way to deal with them.'

Not only Tod's face but his body grew bigger. He was taller, and his shoulders were broader, than before. The heaviness had gone from the air, had become concentrated in the swelling bulk of his chest. There was very little air. The marquee, not more than ten yards off now, seemed as fragile and as dull as burnt-up paper. The tutor was not afraid, was even able to think of Tod with contempt, but he could not move or speak.

'Hit them good and hard – and to do that you've got to organize. Some of us have made a start already. After the Election we decided to form our first Storm detachment down here. Now we've got three detachments. We take our orders from G.H.Q. in London. The party is developing at the rate of about ten thousand new members per week. That isn't generally known, but it soon will be. Before long we shall have the whole country with us – at least all the Englishmen. And we shan't tolerate any passengers in the boat: everyone will have to pull his weight.'

The tutor could not have lifted a finger to protect himself if Tod had decided to hit him, could not have muttered the slightest protest if Tod had commanded him to report at once for Storm duty to the detective. The monstrous bulk of Tod's body dazed him, made him as helpless and lethargic as a frog squatting in the shadow of the expanded hood of a cobra. He could not even find the energy to look once more at the marquee. And now he could see nothing except Tod's face, and he no longer saw that clearly. A huge dim impatience convulsed it, then suddenly it turned away from him. The body became visible again, but this time the tutor was looking at Tod's back. The legs moved with an unnatural, military jerkiness. Tod had abandoned him, was striding towards the detective.

The tutor felt, not relief, but an extreme weakness – as though his last support had been withdrawn from him. He watched Tod approach the detective, saw the two of them walk away together towards the front of the marquee, lost sight of them. He fell forward, it seemed; had the sensation of crawling on his hands and knees. He found himself standing before the side entrance of the marquee. Actually he had walked there, not crawled. He went into the marquee.

He at once felt stronger. He stood still, persuaded himself to focus what was before his eyes, saw a big canvas vaulted space, faintly smoky, at the far end of which groups of people stood talking. The scene was reassuringly normal. Small tables covered with white cloths and surrounded by green iron chairs occupied the central area of uncarpeted grass, and he saw no Nubian statue, no chenille-hung buffalo head. The mild daylight, canvas-enclosed and warmer than it had been outside the marquee, hinted at springtime. But a voice spoke to him, asked him with surprising curtness to show his ticket. He noticed a man sitting at a baize-covered table to the right of the entrance.

'I haven't got one. Can I pay now?'

'Ten shillings.'

The tutor paid without thinking, would have paid ten times as much if he had been asked to and had had the money on him. He refused to allow the man's tone to disturb him. The essential thing now was to avoid over-emphasizing minor impressions. He advanced into the marquee. The grass he walked over was darker and seemed thicker than the grass outside, but that was natural because the light in here was more subdued. On the tables were cut-glass vases filled with daffodils, but slanting iron legs jutting from beneath the borders of the white cloths revealed that the tables were of the ordinary collapsible kind often used in popular tea-gardens. What luxury there was here was only an improvisation. The green iron chairs were collapsible also: a few of them not yet in use were stacked in a pile against the left hand canvas wall of the marquee. A long and high table, covered from top to base with glossy marble-patterned American cloth, was near the stacked chairs, and from behind it rose receding tiers of bottles – golden, ruby, crème de menthe and glinting. But the bottles stood upon a terraced structure of upturned hampers, and he saw a frayed black overcoat hanging from a corner of one of the hampers. Or did he see it? When he looked more carefully the overcoat was not there.

Perhaps the bar-tender had removed it. For the moment, however, no bar-tender was visible, and the tutor did not try to discover one. A little uneasy, he looked away. He quickened his walk, nearly bumped into a small table. A heavy silver bowl, shaped like the head of a lion with a ring through its mouth, was on the table. But he must avoid over-emphasizing his impressions: the bowl was really tin, not silver. And on other tables there were other bowls, also shaped like, no, not like lions' heads but like the heads of other animals – foxes, elephants, stoats. And the tables were laid with white cloths, with brilliant knives, spoons and forks, with intricately folded napkins expanding like white roses from shining tumblers. He reasoned with himself that he must be imagining most of this, that the tables were really quite ordinary. But his reasoning was not convincing. The animal-headed bowls were still there, and they looked more and more like silver. He began to suspect even that he was under-emphasizing his impressions. Perhaps the luxury was quite solid and real, and the frayed black overcoat had been a delusion, had been wilfully imagined by him in his desire to find everything here ordinary. Looking out of the corner of his eye, he became aware again of the terraced bottles. He did not turn to look fully at them, because he suspected now that if he were to do so he would see that the long table was covered not with American cloth but with real marble. And this suspicion disturbed him.

The luxury of the marquee was real, not a mere impression, and in itself it was not unpleasant. True, it was a little remote and superior, made him feel as though he was attending a social function to which he was not quite sure he had been invited. What was disturbing, however, was that the luxury began to remind him of something which had happened just before he had come into the marquee. Something not luxurious but nasty, quite distinct from the silver bowls and the marble and yet having a strange affinity with them – as though the same basic materials had been made up into a different pattern. He refused to be reminded of what had happened. He shut his eyes, opened them, stared straight ahead towards the far end of the marquee. Groups of well-dressed men and women stood easily chatting. He advanced towards them.

'You know what you have to do,' he told himself. Make contact. Find someone whom he recognized, or failing that attach himself unobtrusively to one of the groups. He mustn't expect too much. This was only a beginning. Later there might be yachts and mountains, not today. But he saw no one whom he recognized. Faces comfortably talkative or smilingly rigid, various yet having an unmistakable likeness. Hundreds, some of them sipping drinks. There must be a bar at this end of the marquee also. Clothes various, tweed or formal grey or brilliant, yet with some quality in common. Which group to approach? The nearest. Three well-preserved middle-aged men and one woman. Words, sentences flew out obliquely towards him, made him hesitate.

'And then the old girl crashed down on me from an altitude.... "Oh, Mr Bover!"'

'While all the time Larry was laughing up his sleeve.'

'Excuse me, no.'

'She's a character... Born and bred at Southend.'

'Luckily the M.F.H. popped out of his library just at that moment.'

'Otherwise I'd have been down on my hands and knees – gathering up the fragments that remained.'

'She keeps him in order too.'

'She does.'

What could the tutor contribute to this conversation? Even if he had understood its meaning he would have been quite unable to imitate its tone. So airy it seemed, so detached and musical. The speakers might have been rehearsing for a play. Nevertheless the tutor could not afford to stand still and say nothing. Either he must go forward or he would find himself sliding back. Back to where? He refused to remember, forced himself to open his mouth. But, strain as he might, he could not make a sound. One of the men – Mr Bover? – big-handed and big-hipped, wearing a signet ring, loosely clothed and having the figure of an ex-rugby player, stared him lightly in the face and did not see him.

The tutor remembered Tod. At all costs he must make himself heard. Give up trying to articulate words; to mumble or laugh would be sufficient. Not attempt to assert himself or add anything of his own to their intercourse, but to echo however inefficiently their latest tone. Merge himself in their ritual. They might accept him as an eccentric. Tod must not come back and find him isolated. He smiled, coughed out a laugh. They took no notice. His smile ached horribly. He could not maintain it much longer. But now, from behind them, appeared someone he recognized – the tall man with the puffy face who had been in the first car. The tutor turned the smile on him.

At first the newcomer, like the others, took no notice. Then he saw the tutor and was embarrassed. Suddenly he mastered himself, smiled back. The ache subsided from the tutor's face. The tall man smiled more easily. Eagerly grateful the tutor laughed. The tall man laughed back. They stood facing one another, and the tutor found himself saying without difficulty:

'I saw you in the first car.'

'You were with Ann MacCreath, weren't you?'

'Yes. They picked me up.'

'My name's Gregory Mavors.'

The tutor said quickly:

'I'm the Parkins' tutor.'

Mavors looked keenly at him, but without disapproval; then asked:

'What about a drink?'

'A very good idea.'

They began to walk towards the long marble-patterned table.

'What will you have?'

'I don't know,' the tutor said. 'A stout.'

They approached the table. Its covering, if not of marble, was indisputably of some more solid material than American cloth. And an unlabelled bottle standing on the table contained an opaque golden liquid.

'A stout and a sidecar,' Mavors told the now visible and white-jacketed bar-tender. He said to the tutor: 'How long have you been with the Parkins?'

'About three months.'

'What are they like?'

'Pretty poisonous.'

The tutor immediately wished that he had not said this. Mavors showed no sign of knowing anything about the Parkins, but he seemed to take unfavourable note of the tutor's attitude. He had the interested look of a viva voce examiner who had discovered a gap in a candidate's knowledge. The tutor tried to rehabilitate himself:

'Of course, that's only my own personal view. Anyone who genuinely liked country life, fishing and shooting, might get on very well with them.'

Mavors still had the same look. The tutor picked up a glass of stout which had appeared on the table in front of him. He must not say anything more. But Mavors would not speak either, continued to watch him with the mild waiting stare of a questioner. Awkwardly fascinated the tutor had a sudden wish to commit himself, to confess. He said:

'I suppose I ought never to have taken the job. I'm not suited for it. That's why I called the Parkins poisonous, but I dare say they are quite decent people really.'

Mavors nodded. The tutor felt humiliated, wanted to assert himself again:

'Anyone would seem decent compared with the man I'd just been talking to.'

'Who's he?'

'Tod. I didn't hear his first name. He murdered someone out in Nigeria.'

'Tod Ewan. I know him.'

The inquisitorial look had faded from Mavors' face, was replaced by an interested thoughtfulness. The tutor said with heat:

'He may be lying, of course. Probably he thinks a reputation for murder will make people admire him. But I suspect he wasn't lying when he said he had formed a Storm Troop down here. I saw him talking to a police spy.'

Aware that Mavors was not much impressed, the tutor added more viciously:

'He's loathsomely diseased.'

78

Quietly and almost as though he was beginning to recite a poem, Mavors said:

'Tod Ewan is very ill. He is suffering from malaria and neurosis and on top of these he has had an attack of mob politics. But we have no right yet to describe his condition as loathsome. It may become so in the future, or on the other hand, if he knows how to take it, it may be the prelude of real health such as he has never before experienced.'

'How?' the tutor asked.

'Every disease is a cure if we know the right way to take it. Disease is a result of disobedience to the inner law of our own nature, which works by telling us what we want to do and has no use for "don'ts". From childhood up we are taught that our natural desires are evil, that we must control them, deny them room to grow. But they will not be denied. Twisted, clogged with moralizings, driven back from all normal avenues of development, they nevertheless find a way of asserting themselves, appear in disguise, take on unexpected and abnormal forms – malaria, murder, neurosis, joining a Storm Troop, and whatnot. Yet, even at this stage, there is hope for the sufferer. If only he will abandon Conscious Control. The difficulty for him is to discover which of all the conflicting things within him is Conscious Control and which is Desire, but he will have one sure rule to help him. Desire appears *always* unreasonable.'

'Why?'

The tutor couldn't help being attracted by Mavors. He felt that at last he was listening to someone who was genuinely interested in ideas. Perhaps Mavors was some kind of psychologist. In the same passionately quiet voice Mavors went on:

'Because Desire has been put in prison and driven wild. Consider the case of boys in a preparatory school dormitory, one of whom – Desire – is regarded as strange or bumptious by the rest. They object to his beautiful voice, to the clear ruddy skin of his face, to his dandy pyjamas. They conspire against him, make a combined attack on him, tie him up in a sheet. At first he craftily offers no resistance. Disappointed and a little uneasy they prod and pinch him, and still he does not respond. Then, just as they are about to leave him, he rises up from his bed. Muffled in the sheet he looks like a ghost. They are alarmed, fling themselves on him, try to suffocate him. But somehow he eludes them. Like a competitor in a sack race he goes bounding up the main aisle of the dormitory, makes for the door. They are terrified, plead with him not to be an idiot, tell him they were only joking and that it's all in the day's work. He takes no notice. He comes bounding back towards them. Some of them rush for their beds, try to hide beneath the clothes. But one of them, desperate, clutches at the ghost, tears off the muffling sheet. Desire stands revealed. So great is their relief that they are filled with gratitude towards him. The ringleader even goes up to him and shakes him by the hand, says emotionally – "It was jolly fine the way you took it." And after that evening, Desire is respected and his strangeness taken for granted.'

Mavors sipped his sidecar, gazed hypnotically into the tutor's eyes.

'There is only one sin,' he said, 'and that is disobedience to our desires. It is not our fault, in the first place, that we commit this sin – it is the fault of our early environment and education. The results of this disobedience show themselves in disease and crime – and in hatred, and in regarding the people we live with as "poisonous".'

Mavors made no attempt to pretend that he wasn't thinking of the tutor's attitude towards the Parkins. He went on:

'Disease and hatred are warning symptoms of a sickness of the soul. They come to bring the offenders to their senses. They are Desire in disguise. They are God. And the people who tell us we can "cure" ourselves of them by the exercise of reason and Conscious Control are the Devil. If you cut out a cancer or repress a hatred you will soon develop other symptoms, become a moralist or a dipsomaniac.'

Had the tutor shown a suspicious eagerness in drinking his stout?

'To the sufferer,' Mavors said, 'Conscious Control must always appear noble and right, because the whole natural system has been inverted for him in childhood. He cannot regard Desire otherwise than as something ignoble and wrong. Therefore his salvation lies in being "unreasonable", in rejecting what is "right" and in doing what is "wrong". This can never be easy for him. But if once he succeeds in restoring the natural order he will never turn back. Desire carries its own conviction with it. Life gives nothing richer or lovelier than the moment when, after years of torturing self-control, we at last do what we want to do. When we do, not what we think we ought to do or ought to want to do, but what our nature really wants to do.'

Half amused, half exhilarated, the tutor smiled. He had a moment's misgiving, wondered whether Mavors would be offended, but the misgiving must have been due to Conscious Control. Mavors was frankly pleased, smiled back. He continued to gaze into the tutor's eyes. Intimately, cheekily, his look seemed to ask: 'Do *you* know what you really want to do?' But he said nothing, showed no sign of expecting the tutor to say anything. His enquiring eyes were very close together, as though they were merging their separated gaze into a single mildly searching beam. And this beam penetrated into the tutor's brain, set some mechanism to work there, made him say to himself:

'I know now what I want to do. Since childhood I have deceived myself and been deceived. Even today I have allowed reason to falsify my desires. I have told myself that I wanted a good job and a woman and plenty of upper-middle-class friends, that I wanted to travel, to see mountains, to sail in a yacht. But these things were not what my nature really desired. They were the things that I believed I *ought* to desire. My nature has other, deeper needs. You, Gregory Mavors, have shown me what I want to do. Your love of ideas is my love also. When you speak I am filled with admiration and envy. You are living the life that I have always wanted to live. You are living the truly intellectual life, the life which in my perverse "reasonableness" I have always despised, which I have regarded as a form of affectation and even of prostitution. I was a coward, and I bolstered up my cowardice with the conventional maxims of reason. But you have brought me to my senses. I know now what I shall do. At last, after years of frustration and sloth, I shall begin to use my brain. How dazzling, how lovely my Desire is now that it stands revealed. To study, to become aware of the detail of the world.

Better than piloting an airship, more free than the physical abandon of childhood. And, having opened my eyes and viewed some part of the detail, to retire for a time into thought and there to transform and systematize what I have seen. And then to return to the world, give back to the world the finished product of my thought. And be acclaimed, be welcomed. For they *will* welcome me, even these people here in the marquee, perhaps these more than others. If I have hitherto found them distant, cliquish, superior, that was because my eyesight had been dimmed by the amblyopia of repressed desire. They are better than others, more intelligent, more beautiful. Their smoothness, their comfortable elegance, their musical voices, are signs of culture and goodwill. I shall bring them the dazzling products of my thought, a new, a startling view of history and of anthropology and geology and art, and they will acclaim me. And I know now that I *want* to be acclaimed.'

Mavors seemed to guess what the tutor had been thinking. He said gravely:

'Beware of dabbling in Science.'

'Why?'

'It will lead you back to reason and to Conscious Control. I know that Science looks innocent enough when you first approach it. You will begin by observing a few harmless "facts" about starfish or flowers or domestic animals. Or by picking up a flint arrow-head in a field, or going for a ramble with members of a geological society. But you will not be satisfied with these beginnings. I fancy you are not the type that can patiently spend a lifetime in the collection of facts or specimens. Soon you will turn your attention to human beings. You will learn to regard your body as a mechanism. Even now no irreparable harm will have been done, unless you become interested in medicine or surgery. I need not stress the terrible results which would follow if you were to become convinced that the "irregularities" of the human body can be cured by drugs or by the knife. Let us suppose that you avoid this pitfall, that for the moment you do not follow your mechanistic conception of the body to its logical conclusion. Before long you will find yourself applying this same conception to the human situation in general – to the "body

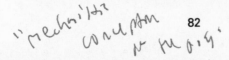

politic" as no doubt you will call it. You will examine social conditions and discover that they are morbid. You will diagnose poverty, malnutrition, overcrowding, injustice and crime. And now reason will come into its own. It will show you a future black with horror, will prove beyond dispute that there can be no escape, that conditions must steadily worsen, unrest grow, starvation and tyranny advance, and finally that war will deluge the whole world with blood. Poisoned inwardly by these ideas you will become shifty and timid in your outward behaviour. The people you most want to make friends with, the beautiful, the cultured, the happy and the free, will intuitively recoil from you. And in the end you will not even be allowed the consolation of exercising your brain. So grim a picture of the future will reason have painted for you that thought itself will begin to appear futile to you. The disease of reason will have run its course, and you will sink into a final coma. Or if, by a last effort, you continue to think, your thinking will be a mere echo of the shrill and sterile slogans of one of the new mob-militant political movements.'

The tutor, in spite of his exhilaration and his admiration for Mavors, couldn't help raising an objection:

'But if the world situation is in actual fact getting worse every day I don't see how I could save myself from it merely by rejecting reason. War would still maim or kill me, however promptly I obeyed the voice of Desire. Or do you believe that war and starvation and tyranny are only figments of reason and that they don't really exist?'

Mavors was surprised at the tutor's stupidity.

'Of course they exist,' he said. 'But not as reason makes them appear to us. And if you apply Conscious Control to them you will make them even worse than they are already. If you demolish a slum in one part of a city you will create a far larger slum in another part. If you try to stop a war in Asia you will give a fillip to civil war in Europe. And if then you introduce measures of "reasonable" reform into a crown colony you will evoke an orgy of blind assassination. Because poverty and war and slavery and all the social evils of our time are themselves the result of disobedience to Desire. In our hearts we *want* to be well-off and free and to live at peace with our neighbours, but we *reason* with ourselves that our bank accounts or our employers or our neighbours will prevent us from getting what we want. So we throttle our desires within us and consciously try to adapt ourselves to the outer world as reason views it. But Desire will not be throttled, returns to us in sinister disguises, drives us to acts of degradation and violence. Starvation and war begin to advance across the world. And at this stage, if you try to "cure" the world with further doses of reason and Control, the result will be universal Death.'

Mavors stared into the tutor's eyes, added: 'Give your Desire room to grow. Don't tell yourself – "I can't". You can – and all these obstacles which reason has conjured up before you will fall away like straw.'

The tutor still had his doubts:

'If I have got to reject reason how am I going to use my brain? That is what I really want to do.'

'Put the question to yourself in another way: "If I cling to reason how am I going to use my brain?" Reason is death, destroys the mind as well as the body. Without unreason there can be no thought.'

'But what is the nature of unreason? I mean, if it just seems a blank to me I can't very well use my brain on it.'

'Unreason is the language of desire. Years of patient study would not help even the most brilliant linguist to understand a single word of it. If you are to master it you must first of all release your Desire from prison. As soon as you have done this you will find yourself speaking it like a native. You want to make friends with these people here in the marquee, to admire and be admired by them. Very well: go up and introduce yourself. Don't let reason persuade you that you will be snubbed or that you will not be able to add anything of interest to their conversation. Speak. Don't be put out when reason warns you that what you are saying to them is fantastic or impertinent. Remember that whatever seems "wrong" to your conscious mind is, according to the inner law of your nature, right. And though at first they, too, may be deceived by reason and may try to ignore you, their Desire will recognize the authentic voice of yours and in the end they will respond to you with deepest gratitude.'

The tutor said:

'I know what my Desire is; and I think I know now what unreason is, but I doubt whether it would give me any intellectual satisfaction. It seems negative, the mere contradiction of reason. What concrete data has unreason to work on?'

Mavors may or may not have answered this question. The tutor did not listen. Before he had finished speaking he had himself found an answer. His attention, possibly because Mavors was no longer staring into his eyes, had strayed to the unlabelled bottle on the marble-patterned table. Mavors may or may not have been looking at it too. The tutor wasn't sure. The opaque liquid in the bottle had all the brightness of solid brass. An excitement surged up like a rocket within the tutor. He understood now what concrete materials unreason would work on. This bottle and this table and the animal-headed bowls and the white silk table-cloths – these were the data of unreason. These he would study, would know in their every detail, would analyse and develop and transform within his mind, would give back in startling images to the world from which he had taken them. He would give them back to the people in the marquee, and he would be acclaimed. These were the things he would speak of when he introduced himself. But mightn't it be dangerous to speak of them, dangerous even to think of them? He looked at a silver bowl on one of the small tables, saw that it was moulded to represent a squirrel. No, not moulded; its detail was far too clear-cut and intricate. Every hair of the curving tail must have been modelled separately. The figure as a whole had nothing impressionistic about it, did not suggest that more was meant by it than had been visibly expressed. It was unambiguously pleasant, was what he desired it to be. Certainly if he were to look at it now through the eyes of reason it would soon become ambiguous and disturbing, would begin to remind him of Tod. But never again would he allow reason to stultify his Desire. He had wanted Tod to be friendly, to be a hero and a pioneer, but his reason had argued that Tod could not really be like this, and consequently his Desire, driven wild by the opposition of reason, had made Tod someone dangerous, a reactionary and an enemy. He had wanted the people in the marquee to welcome him, but he had reasoned that they would not do so, and therefore his Desire, poisoned by reason, had made them aloof and superior. He had wanted the bowls on the tables to be silver, and his Desire, freed at last from reason, had made them silver. Now, having learnt his lesson, he would look again at the people in the marquee, would see them this time through the eyes of unreason, and they would become what he desired them to become.

He looked boldly at the group which had ignored him a few minutes before. He saw no immediate danger in them: their postures, their gestures were much the same now as then. The ex-rugby player was still elegantly talking, chin in air, elbow bent backwards and forward and fingers resting with artificial ease on a tweed-clothed thigh. The woman, permanently smiling, blinked her eyelids in rapid little signals of amazed assent. The faces of the two male listeners, less demonstratively amused, were turned towards the woman and at right angles to each other, had an almost identical expression of pleased inquiry – as though one had been an oblique mirror reflection of the other. But as the tutor stared at them the two men began to lose confidence in their pose, to grow restive. The woman also – in spite of her ever-increasing effort to appear remote and theatrical, of her flickering eyelashes imitating the waving antennae of an insect – was becoming more genuinely animated, more human. An uncontrollable tremor – perhaps of alarm, perhaps of delighted expectancy – disturbed her posing face and rippled down her body. And then the ex-rugby player, in the middle of achieving an exquisitely superior airy gesture with his cocktail glass, turned his head and looked at the tutor. The look was one of entire surrender, of friendly awe. The tutor had come to power. In a moment he would be among them, would begin to deliver the message they were waiting for. Words, colours, tunes, all he knew and felt about the decorations here, about the squirrel, the bright brass bottle, the table-cloths. What words? Already he imagined himself saying: 'A gilded cinema organ might I think embellish.' He would not say that, perhaps: unreason would furnish him, when the moment came for him to speak, with words far richer than any he could now imagine. How he would dazzle, charm, bewilder these people; and then he would leave them. He would advance, win other and fuller recognition, would extend his power to the farthest limits of the marquee. He would extend it even to the people now standing by the main entrance of the marquee, though that might be less easy.

Tod had just come in through the main entrance. He was no longer in the company of the detective, and his serious red face did not appear in any way alarming. Nevertheless, his presence had introduced a doubt into the tutor's enthusiastic train of thought. Unreason might have, certainly did have, power to change inanimate objects, but would it always succeed with human beings, with conscious objects who might themselves choose to reason and to ignore the voice of his Desire? The tutor must have expressed this doubt aloud, for Mavors said:

'The man who has released his Desire will always prevail over the man who tries to keep his Desire is chains. And the explanation of this is simple: the man who reasons is divided against himself, and the more vital part of him, his Desire, must take the side of his unreasoning opponent, of the man whose Desire is free. Therefore your power to change human beings will be no less than your power to change inanimate objects.'

The tutor was ready to believe it. However, before he could be quite sure that Mavors was right, he must look once again at Tod. But Tod was no longer standing at the main entrance, was not to be seen anywhere, must have mixed with the crowd in the marquee. His disappearance somehow suggested a new doubt to the tutor, who said aloud:

'But suppose one man converts another to unreason – might not the other's released Desire come into conflict with the Desire of the converter?'

'No. Conflict is a product of reason. Unrepressed Desire is always lively and friendly. What's good for you – good in the profoundest sense – can never be bad for another person.'

The tutor thought: 'But does it follow that what's good for another person will be good for me?' He said:

'Was it good for the Nigerian native when Tod Ewan shot him?'

Mavors had a look of impatience. Controlling himself he said slowly, like a schoolmaster to a very stupid boy:

'Of course not. Nor was it good for Tod. Think – why did he do it? Because he *desired* to bring about a death? Is that the answer? No. Desire creates life, only reason brings death. He listened to reason, and reason told him that he was in a foreign country, that he was there not as a guest but as a usurper, as an exploiter whom the Hausa natives must wish to be rid of; and so his Desire to be happy and friendly was distorted by reason into a suspicion, a distrust, and finally into a certainty that the native in question had designs against his life. Even now murder might have been avoided – if only the native had been unreasonable. But he, too, was affected by the same virus; he, too, reasoned that Tod was an intruder, and so his nature Desire to be friendly and happy became – '

Mavors stopped, apparently in order to sip his cocktail. The tutor said:

'I understand what you mean. Conflict can only arise when *both* parties to it are poisoned by reason. I suppose you would say the same about international war: if one side behaved unreasonably then war could never break out. Or if one country behaved unreasonably war couldn't break out. Or even if a few individuals in one country. . . . But how many individuals? Ten or eleven wouldn't be enough. They couldn't influence the decisive mass of reasonable people, because they would come in contact with too few of them. What's the minimum number of unreasonable people required if Desire is to be effective in the world as a whole? And can we get them – shall we get them in time?'

Mavors sipped his cocktail, said nothing, did not appear to have been paying much attention to what the tutor had said. But the tutor had found his own solution to the problem he had raised. With conviction, with enthusiasm he went on:

'We may not get them in time. But we can and must try to get them. It is the only hope. You have taught me that, Gregory Mavors. I shall remember it. And already I have succeeded in winning over some of the people here. I shall go on, and I shall win over others.'

Mavors looked pleased. But he was not looking at the tutor. He waved his cocktail glass and grinned. And now the tutor understood why Mavors had stopped speaking. Tod had reappeared out of the crowd and was walking towards them. Making his way between the tables in the middle of the marquee – a short cut which involved him in clumsily pushing chairs out of his way – he called out to Mavors:

'Looking for you all over the place.'

Mavors called back:

'When in doubt try the bar.'

Tod came up to them, his face beaming, and Mavors asked him:

'What are you having?'

'No, thanks. There isn't time. I wanted a word with you. Something you ought to know.'

His face beamed, gleamed like a varnished mask, but his eyes were serious.

He ignored the tutor.

'What is it?' Mavors asked.

Tod took him by the elbow, urged him away from the bar. Mavors hesitated, glanced back for a moment at the tutor, said indecisively:

'Why not here?'

Tod answered with an abrupt shake of the head. He led Mavors away.

The tutor tried not to feel insulted. 'Be unreasonable,' he told himself. He thought of the unlabelled bottle and the silver squirrel. He stared at the bottle. The liquid inside it was still as bright as brass. Reassured, he turned his head and looked at the squirrel. It was silver, in no way changed. But why did it give him the feeling that he must not take his eyes off it? Wrong: this feeling came from another source, from something that he suspected was happening at the far end of the marquee. The squirrel, properly regarded, was a guarantee that what was now happening beyond it would also be amenable to unreason, could also be made pleasant. Danger lay only in refusing to look beyond.

He looked.

Near the main entrance Humphrey Silcox stood facing a group of about twenty young men. A few girls, apart from the main group, were watching. The men, bunched closely together, were not talking. They were waiting. Silcox signalled to them with a

casual wave of his hand. They moved smartly into line, formed
two ranks, stood at attention. He numbered them. Their behaviour caused no visible surprise among the other people near
them. On the contrary, there seemed a tendency for the men
elsewhere in the marquee to imitate them, to stand more stiffly.
And now Silcox had raised his arm in the fascist salute. His men
saluted also. Tod, arriving with Mavors, returned the salute. He
said something to Silcox, and Mavors then walked over to the
group, attached himself at the end of the rear rank, stood at
attention. Mavors had not saluted, and he did not look altogether
sure of himself now. The tutor regarded the scene as wholly
ridiculous, a comic game. But he was unable to sustain his
amusement for long: against his will he began to feel bored.
These antics weren't even really funny. His gaze shifted back
again to the unlabelled bottle. That at least was interesting. He
noticed that there were other people standing quite near him at
the bar. They were drinking and talking: there was nothing
unnatural about them. They weren't on parade. But why had the
parade at the far end of the marquee seemed boring? Because he
had allowed himself to think of it reasonably. Boredom was bad,
should not be tolerated. Tod and Silcox and the young men were
behaving unreasonably, and therefore they were in fact interesting. It was up to the tutor to view them unreasonably, and then
they would seem interesting. He must try again.

Tod was making a speech. Broad-backed and stiff, fists on
hips, elbows jutting sideways like the heavy handles of a fat
earthenware jug. The rigidity of his body gave additional
emphasis to the violent activity of his face. His chin prodded out
towards the listening young men, reached so far that the tutor
wondered why his body didn't bend or overbalance. His lips gob-
bled, pouted to a pause, flapped open again, and moved even
faster than before. The young men listened with expressionless
faces. At intervals they mechanically clapped. Mavors clapped,
too, but his face was not expressionless. He looked uncomfortable. The tutor noticed that people elsewhere in the marquee
were listening also. The speech was having its effect even on the
group of four who had just previously been ready to welcome
him. There were signs that they were becoming aloof and superior

once again. He was losing his influence over them. Quick, reassert himself, back to the attack, plunge deeper still into unreason.

He began to hear what Tod was saying.

'Our observers have kept us well supplied with information. The first report to come in this morning left us in no doubt at all as to what was afoot. . . . Number five noticed suspicious activity on the part of a steam-roller driver. Also, a hostile demonstration by women in a motor coach. . . . A large section of the crowd, carrying rucksacks and armed with sticks, was seen to cut across the road and to climb towards the racecourse under cover of trees. We are in possession of the names of the leaders. As was to be expected, all of them came from outside the district and the majority from abroad. I have received photographs of them and these will be passed round before we leave the marquee. . . . The position is serious, but less so than it was two months ago. We recognize that this plot is a sign of desperation. . . . Having failed to ruin the M.F.H. by financial trickery, they are resorting to criminal violence. . . . International Jewry – '

Tod was interrupted by a burst of jeering laughter. But the young men were not, as the tutor momentarily hoped, laughing at Tod: they were applauding him. They believed every word he said. Or, at least, their negative devitalized faces showed no glimmer of disbelief. Tod went on:

'They'll be looking pretty yellow by the time we've finished with them. . . . It won't take us long. . . . Just a spot of bother. . . . The police will co-operate. . . . This plot is the signal we have been waiting for. At last the criminal forces have come into the open. They have thrown off the humanitarian, peace-loving, progressive disguises with which they hoped to fool the more sentimental and woolly-minded of our fellow-countrymen. . . . It is our privilege today to strike a blow for all that is best in the national heritage. For honour, for the spirit, for idealism, for everything that makes life worth while. Against the cowardly hypocrisy of politicians, against disloyalty, against money-grubbing materialism, against the selfishness of the profiteering employer, against the whining discontent of the socialistic trade unionist. . . . To restore the moral fibre of our nation. . . . We shall not falter. . . . '

The young men clapped and cheered. The girls cheered also, but less loudly – as though they were afraid of appearing unladylike. Mr Bover clapped, and the woman, and the other two men. Even the people standing near the tutor at the bar seemed to approve of the speech. For an instant the tutor felt that he, too, if he tried hard enough, might be able to approve, or at least to prevent himself from disapproving. He must try to remember that this parade was only a game, a charade of unreason. It was a game, and he, too, could play it. But did he want to play it? Would it enable him to realize his profoundest desire, give him scope to use his brain? He might continue to *think* about the silver squirrel and the unlabelled bottle, but he would have to *talk* about abstract colourless words like 'romance' and 'the spirit'. Or worse, he might have to stand at attention and listen carefully while Tod gave orders. He wouldn't be able to think for himself at all, not even unreasonably. And suppose he refused to play Tod's game, suppose he attached himself to some other group in the marquee – would he be any less restricted? The other people here – even those who had not applauded Tod's speech – were every moment becoming more interested in the parade of the young men. There was no escape anywhere here for the tutor. He would never be able to use his brain, would never be acclaimed.

It was futile, dangerous to allow himself to become alarmed. He knew he would never be a poet or a prophet, but that didn't mean he was done for, a hopeless failure. There were other, humbler ways of living a happy life. What ways? Where? Not outside the marquee, not by going back to the house he had come from this morning. The happier life must be here or nowhere, must be among these people here. But they were becoming more and more aloof, even those who stood nearest to the tutor and who had been least impressed by Tod. They looked colder and older, devitalized: their sociable movements, head-noddings and hand gesturings, were weary and sluggish, seemed to arise no longer from their own volition but to be compelled by some external influence. Even their expensive clothes had begun to look dowdy and colourless. And the flesh of their faces, in the faintly green light reflected from the grass, was dusty grey, like the flesh of dead goldfish. The tutor knew that he would never succeed in making contact with these people. They were as inaccessible to the language of his wishes as the dead in a cemetery or the imagined inhabitants of Mars. He was isolated, lost, perhaps for ever.

He was no longer able to control his alarm. 'Perhaps I am done for,' he thought. But as he thought this someone stared at him. A girl standing quite near him at the bar. At first he dared not return the stare, because he was afraid he might discover that he had been mistaken. But the girl continued to stare. She moved towards him. Her fingers, holding a cocktail glass, slid along the marble edge of the bar. She was wearing a fur coat and a blue scarf. He looked up at her face and saw it animated with recognition and pleasure.

'You don't remember me,' she said.

'Yes. I saw you in the first car.'

'You saw me at least six years before that.'

'I think.... I'm not sure.'

'Think again.'

'One evening. At Cambridge.'

'In the street. You were wearing a black gown, but you looked like a faun. I pretended I wanted to escape. I hurried down a dark alley by one of the colleges. You followed me and I came to a stop on the grass against some railings. I was only nineteen and I was very excited. You talked about mountains.'

'Did I?'

Disturbed, he forced himself to add casually:

'What happened then?'

'You played with the fur of my gloves. It was rabbit's fur. There was frost on the railings and on the grass. You talked about pergolas and about fountains. I had never heard that sort of language spoken before, but I knew at once that I had always wanted to hear it. I remember one phrase specially: "Rubber statuary in gardens of ice-cream roses." It made me laugh – really laugh, not just giggle in the way I had always done when other men had made jokes for my benefit. I nearly cried. Your talk was like some marvellous poem, and you never hesitated for a word. I think you realized how much I appreciated what you

93

were saying. You got better and better as you went on. And when you told me you had never been so lucky with any girl before, I believed you.'

Her eyes, bright white and dark brown, were warm with frank desire. But he refused to allow their warmth to invade him. He must see her quite dispassionately – a beautiful dummy with icy ear-rings and a face cool as a frozen peach. And her voice was warm:

'I agreed to meet you next evening outside a cinema. I've forgotten the name of the cinema but I remember exactly where it was.'

'The Rendezvous.'

Her face moved towards his, and he had an impulse to add: 'Why didn't you come?' But he warned himself that if he showed any interest in her she might begin to find him less attractive. She said:

'Then I asked you whether you had been drinking.'

'I had, of course.'

'I might never have noticed it if I hadn't kissed you. I suppose you guessed it would make a bad impression, and that's why you tried to keep your face away from mine. And when I'd found you out you told me that you hadn't drunk very much.'

'I'd seldom drunk more.'

You tried to convince me that it made no difference and that your feeling for me would be just the same the next day. You pleaded with me to let you prove that you were telling the truth. You made me promise twice that I wouldn't fail to meet you outside the cinema. I swore I would come, but you knew I was only humouring you. Then you told me you would give anything not to have been drinking, that in the morning you would realize to the full what I was and what you had lost.'

He heard himself say:

'That was quite true.'

'I know it was. I knew it then. But I had made up my mind earlier in the evening that I would never again have anything to do with any man who got drunk. Oh, how can I have been such a fool? All because I had just had a quarrel with Humphrey. What a hateful little prig I must have been.'

94

He was surprised into asking anxiously:

'Do you mean Humphrey Silcox?'

'Yes.'

She controlled a smile, added quickly:

'I had decided never to see him again. His friends always disgusted me, and that evening I felt there was nothing to choose between him and them. All they could do was to drink and tell dirty stories. They were terribly boring. I suddenly lost my temper and walked out of the room. Humphrey was doing a tap-dance on the fender. He ran after me, but I told him he made me sick. He didn't ask why – he just got frightfully angry. That was typical of him. I walked out into the street. Soon afterwards I met you.'

Her face moved nearer to his. Her lips were trembling.

'I realized at once that you were different from the others, but when I discovered that you had been drinking too I made up my mind I wouldn't meet you next day. I didn't turn up at the cinema. It was sheer obstinacy. I have never forgiven myself.'

She tilted her head backwards, took a deep breath, sighed with theatrical regret. Her half-closed eyelids fluttered. Her full, rouged lips pouted wooingly. Her face was very young. He knew that she was play-acting, but she acted with such confidence and vitality, with such whole-hearted indifference to the other people standing near her at the bar, that he couldn't help admiring her. He was no longer able to check the feeling of warmth that was increasing within him. Nevertheless he was determined that she should not see what he felt. He waited for her to speak again. She said:

'Afterwards I knew that you were the first person I'd met in my life who had made me really happy. You were the first, and there's been no one like you since then.'

She whispered, moaned. Her eyes were closed, her head dropped backwards, surrendering, waiting for him to bend over her. He did not move. Her eyes slowly opened again, tried to discover what impression her behaviour had made on him, were puzzled. Displeasure or apprehension for a moment disturbed her deliberately yearning face. She had become aware of the possibility of defeat. But a new, a final tactic occurred to her.

Still looking at him, she moved away from him, stepped quickly backwards, tense and agile as a dancer. Her hands rose towards her throat, gripping the edges of her fur coat. The coat fell open, exposing a silk-covered bosom. Her small blue scarf pointed downwards between her breasts. He was not deceived, knew without the least doubt that her action was a deliberate trick. But there was no trickery, nothing artificial, about what she had to show him. Slowly she arched her back, and her large rigid breasts swelled out towards him, seemed to force aside the heavy edges of her coat. With softness and yet with unhesitating strength they rose, like young plants pushing up through heavy soil. They burst into silky blossom, mauve shot with orange. Impudently they pointed sideways, their clearly defined nipples like ogling eyes. They were solid and hostile as fists, yet soft as down. Their brutal rigidity assaulted and wounded him, yet they were divided and meekly offered themselves to him. Warmth spurted up within him like the spurting of a hot spring. In an instant he decided to surrender. 'Let it gush out,' he thought. No matter how foolish or how dangerous. He would deliver himself over to her. He said:

'I waited more than an hour. Then I walked up and down the main streets, looking for you. I was in despair. And the next night I looked for you again. You were the first girl I had been genuinely attracted to, had admired without reservations. I was in love with you. I still am.'

As he spoke he became more confident. He would conquer her, not sacrifice himself to her. He would penetrate her pretences, seize hold of her genuine beauty. She said mildly:

'I am in love with you, too. We were born for each other.'

Triumph deepened the colour of her face, and tears came into her eyes. Mildly she added:

'I have never been able to make Humphrey understand... how I felt towards you.'

Shock made him ask sharply:

'What's Humphrey got to do with it?'

'I'm engaged to him. Didn't I tell you?'

He was aware that he had lost control of the muscles of his face. He tried to be angry, to show contempt, but his disappointment overpowered him, exhibited itself to her in wretched nakedness. She made an effort not to laugh at him, said with excessive sympathy:

'Oh, but darling, it will make no difference. You must believe me. I could never feel the same about Humphrey as I do about you.'

She had to laugh. Her voice rose in a trill of genuine delight. Quickly, primly, she checked herself. Her small fist thumped against her silk-covered collar-bone. Tragically she said:

'I ought not to have become engaged to him. I do feel such a swine. What bitches women are. I don't know why I did it. You are the only man I've ever cared for.'

She had conquered her amusement. Her tone of tragic passion became more assured:

'I cannot believe that it's too late. We will go away together. We will live together. In a golden land. Among the pergolas and the fountains. You will come with me, won't you, my sweet?'

He stared at her in an unhappy stupor. She jumped towards him. Regardless of other people at the bar she put her arm round his neck, pushed her lips against his mouth. His lips responded; weakly at first, then with increasing pleasure. He began to move to the attack, to kiss with vigour. Immediately she withdrew her lips from his. Her arms slid slowly away from his neck and across his shoulder, her body detached itself from him with the precise ease of some potent perfectly controlled machine. She stared calmly at his face, watched its new confidence lapse into protest, into dejection, into abasement. Then, as though judging him finally tamed, she put her arm round his neck once more, pressed softly against him, kissed. This time he did not try to move to the attack, did not even try to defend. His nerves, his body, responded to her slavishly, her bosom crowded against his chest; her lips pressed, withdrew until their touch seemed as light as the touch of an insect's trembling feelers, pressed again, sucking and warm and heavy. He was in her power, wholly dependent on her, humbled with abject longing. After a while she released him, stepped back. She watched him, waited like some brilliant dangerous insect till the delicious poison she had injected should begin to take its full effect.

He began to speak:

'I can't do without you.'

'There's no need for you to do without me.'

'How soon can we live together?'

'As soon as you like. Tomorrow. Next week. What does time matter to us?'

She was entirely calm. He said:

'But time does matter to me. I can't help it. I don't know what I should do if I had to wait.'

She gave a flattered, superficial little laugh, said:

'Let's go now, at once.'

'Yes, I'm sick of this place. Let's get away. We can decide later where we'll go.' He hesitated. 'But I suppose I ought to find Mr Parkin and tell him I'm not coming back. Otherwise he might – no, why should I tell him? Serve him right.' He hesitated again. 'But you'll want to go home first and collect your things.'

She was laughing again.

'What a practical little man you are.'

'Am I? I only thought – I mean, if we're going away, you'll want to pack some clothes, won't you?'

Gaily she raised her arms from her sides, made a gesture of careless freedom.

'No. I don't want us to make any preparations. That would spoil it all. I want to fly. I feel I could fly through the air now like a swallow – or a swan.'

She waved her arms like wings.

'All right. Where shall we fly to?'

'Anywhere. Everywhere. Honolulu. London. Now. Just as we are. Cape Wrath. Better still – Reykjavik.'

Her words jerked him out of the satisfying trance into which he had begun to sink. He tried and failed to remember where he had heard them before. He looked at her face and was certain of one thing – that she was not jeering at him. She was waiting without impatience, with confidence, for him to speak, for him to add something new to her daydream. She was unmistakeably sincere. Her face had a genuine innocence, was like the face of a child who is preoccupied with playing an exciting imaginative game. If only he could discover what her words reminded him of, then perhaps he, too, would be able to enter whole-heartedly into the game, would be able to feel happy. But he found difficulty in concentrating his thoughts. He was becoming aware once again of the people at the far end of the marquee. He tried not to look at them, but they increasingly forced themselves upon his attention. The young men, as before, stood in ranks on either side of the main entrance. Now, however, their faces were not altogether expressionless, showed a stolid exaltation, were upturned towards the top half of the entrance as though they expected to see appear there at any moment the head of an abnormally tall man. A whisper arose from among them, faint and prolonged, like the hiss of water in a remote cistern. Tod glanced very briefly along the ranks, then turned again to stare towards the entrance. The whisper began to spread among the crowd. Slowly it approached the tutor, resolved itself into audible words:

''Scumming. 'Scumming. 'Scoming. He's coming. He's coming. He's coming.'

He looked at the girl in front of him, saw that she, too, had heard. With mild interest she said:

'I suppose it's the M.F.H.'

Her face gave no hint of uneasiness or enthusiasm. Soon she had ceased to pay any attention to the whisper. She was looking steadily at him, waiting for him to make the next move in her daydream game. Now, more than ever, she appeared to him childish and innocent. Her vices – her teasing and her posing – no longer seemed important, were even charming. Against the dangerous background of the whispering crowd she had for him something of the pathos of a very young and good-looking woman naively exhibiting herself at a commercialized beauty competition. Afterwards the millionaire judges would auction her among themselves. Silcox would get her. Tod and the whisperers would crudely strip her of all her charm. She was weak and ignorant, without the least suspicion of what was being prepared for her behind her back. Yet she was strong, too. She stood looking at him upright and without moving, her back towards the crowd and the ugly preparations, undisturbed, powerful with young dignity, with beauty no longer aphrodisiac, with simple joy. Silcox and Tod would never get her. She was stronger than they were. They had violence and conviction, but in the end they would destroy themselves, perish in their own ugliness. They would perish because they were fighting against nature and humanity, were fighting against themselves. She, or others like her, would survive because she was on the side of the forces of life, and those forces would survive. But was the tutor himself on the side of life? Would he get her? That was the crucial uncertainty. He began to understand the meaning of what she had said about Reykjavik. He could not remember yet where he had heard her words before, but he knew now what they implied – uncertainty. They were words in the air, cloudy daydream words, nothing more than words. It was necessary for him to bring them down to earth, to make her define them in terms of real life: otherwise he would lose her. He could not afford to lose her. He knew that she was his last chance of joy. More, she was the only valid joy; all other pleasures – travel, using his brain, poetry, making new friends – were, even if they had still been possible for him, profoundly inferior. With love and amazement he looked at her, thought: 'She is a human being, has feelings like mine.' Yet, in every feature she seemed his opposite, as foreign to him as though she were some lovely mythical animal. A minute chemical difference in the hormones, and this unique wonder had arisen. He was not going to lose her. The joy and splendour of life. No matter what she demanded of him. He would even wear a top hat, accompany her to social tea-parties, have the baby christened, live in a house with servants to wait on him, travel daily by car to the office. He would get her, bring her down to earth, make her declare herself – yes or no. Otherwise –

But she seemed to have a premonition of what he was going to tell her. And as though she wished to fend him off she said airily:

'Definitely we must go to Reykjavik.'

He said:

'I want to marry you.'

Her face changed with the abruptness of a lantern-slide. From dreaminess to business. She laughed slightly, but her laugh, for the first time since the beginning of their encounter, was forced.

'Oh, but darling, you are far too nice to marry.'

'Why?'

'I don't want to hurt your feelings, my sweet, but really' – her amusement became a little more genuine – 'I simply can't picture you as the earnest breadwinner supporting a wife and family.'

'I don't propose to be an earnest breadwinner. And I know that if I went on being a tutor I couldn't hope to support a wife and family. But this afternoon I've had the offer of a really good job.'

She was visibly startled, she hesitated, then said firmly:

'No, it's impossible. I only wish we could.'

'Why is it impossible?'

'Darling, you're not the marrying sort.'

'And I suppose Humphrey Silcox is the marrying sort.'

'Yes, he is. I wish you could understand. I feel quite differently towards him. I am much more, more *passive* with him than with you. With you I feel an extraordinary tenderness, my heart melts when I look at you. I feel all protective. I can't imagine you keeping a wife in order, darling. And women are such bitches. I do wish I could make Humphrey understand what I feel about you. He's so jealous. I adore you.'

'I love you.'

'I adore you. I know I ought to marry you and not him. What a fool I am. We were made for each other.'

Her face showed a genuine indecision, but he guessed that if he were to mention marriage again she would harden against him. He must wait for her to make the next move. It was not easy to wait. Apprehension, misery, were beginning to take hold of him. Soon he would lose control over them, she would see what he felt and his chances of getting her would be ruined finally. It was difficult to control them, because they gained impetus not only from her attitude towards him but also from the behaviour of the other people in the marquee. The whisper which the young men had started had deepened into a murmur. An ugly enthusiasm was spreading everywhere. He dared not wait any longer.

'We needn't be married. We can live together.' Her look made him add. 'I mean, we can go *away* together for a time.'

'Yes.' Instantly she changed her mind: 'I don't know. A few

minutes ago I shouldn't have hesitated. But I had no idea then that you took it so seriously.'

'I'll take it whatever way you want me to take it.'

'No. It wouldn't work. You would feel even more wretched afterwards than you do now.'

'I don't feel wretched now.'

The murmur had become louder. He pleaded:

'We can't know that it wouldn't work until we've tried it. Come away with me for one night.'

'No, darling. I've been swine enough already. I don't want to become even worse.'

He made a last attempt.

'Let's go to Reykjavik.'

But even that daydream pretence had ceased to appeal to her. She didn't bother to answer him. The murmur grew louder and louder. She turned her head away from him, looked towards the main entrance of the marquee. Suddenly, with a simple delighted laugh, she said: 'Well, I never, if that isn't Humphrey parading over there. How frightfully funny he looks.'

'I can't do without you.'

With an effort she brought her attention back to the tutor.

'You needn't do without me, darling. I wish you would understand. I adore you. We ought never to have made the mistake of getting our relationship mixed up with sex. You are really something much more to me than just a lover. I feel I can talk to you – about anything I like. I don't feel that when I'm with Humphrey. You are good for me.' She paused to find the right words. 'It's so difficult to explain. You see, I don't think of you exactly as a man. You are more like a girl friend. Or a faun. You are someone I can be really happy with.'

Abjectly he said:

'Promise at least that you won't abandon me.'

'Of course I won't abandon you.'

The noise in the marquee was no longer a murmur: it was almost a roar. Like the subdued roar of the draught in a newly lighted stove. She was again looking at Humphrey. Smiling, she said:

'I think I ought to go over and talk to him. He'll begin to get jealous if I don't. I'll come back to you later.' She gave the tutor a glad stare, then added earnestly: 'You mustn't look so miserable. I don't like it.'

He weakly tried to control his face.

'You poor little swine,' she said.

She turned and, with a hint of disapproval in her final glance at him, walked away.

He soon lost sight of her. The increasing noise confused him, blurred all his feelings, affected even his vision. Now he saw nothing distinctly – except the opaque golden bottle on the marble bar. The sight of it was his only support: if it disappeared anything might happen to him, he would fall down, lose consciousness altogether. But it did not disappear. Very gradually his field of vision began to expand, he saw again the nearer tables, the animal-headed silver bowls. The noise increased to a roar, vaulted into a bellow of cheering. The bowls had an evil look, like objects in a devil temple. They were something more than quaint ornaments: they had a definite connection with the nasty ritual which was being performed at the other end of the marquee. The cheering grew louder and louder. All at once – with the icy clearness which comes in instants of danger, which comes in the fraction of a second before a traffic accident or a blow from a baton – he saw exactly what was happening. The M.F.H. was walking into the marquee through the main entrance. He was abnormally short, and his face had an exhausted look, but there was nothing else unusual about him. Perfunctorily he raised his arm in reply to the rigid salutes of the young men. He stopped walking. Slowly the cheering subsided. He, or someone else – possibly Tod or Silcox – the tutor couldn't be sure – began to speak. Most of the words were inaudible, but now and again a phrase or a sentence reached the tutor so clearly and loudly that it might have come from an amplifier hanging within a few yards of his ear.

'...Fritillary will run today....'

The cheering, which had not yet entirely ceased, now bellowed out once again. As it dwindled anew, the tutor heard:

'...The threatened strike has been called off. Not a moment too soon....'

Mad cheering. People were jumping about in their enthusiasm. Even the young men were agitated, were beginning to break out of their ranks. Among the enthusiasts the tutor noticed Mr Parkin. He was hysterically capering, prancing, thumping the backs of his neighbours in the crowd. The sight did not disgust the tutor, gave him no feelings at all. He was without feelings, and might have remained so if he had not suddenly seen Dorothy MacCreath. She was dancing a Highland fling. He had no sooner recognized her than he recognized, one by one, the men and girls he had seen in the first car. Of all those who had seemed so admirable, so free and happy, only Ann was not here, was not cheering. And now, in retrospect, their freedom and their happiness had an odious fraudulence which made them appear far more ugly, more brutally stupid, than any of the other people in the marquee. The tutor felt a sick despair, began to be really afraid. The voice went on:

'...I am at liberty now to tell you the whole truth.... It has been a very close thing indeed.... Our untiring vigilance.... Their object was first of all to paralyse transport and the mines, and thus to cripple our munitions industry.... The docks.... Their agents.... The police were able to make a number of important arrests early this morning.... A mere question of hours before we get the others.... With your co-operation.... It is a very great victory.... No cause for complacency.... We have smashed the internal attack and now we may expect the external.... At any moment.... Yes.... Thank God we are in a better condition to face it than we were, than we should have been if.... But we are not yet out of the wood.... The common effort of a united nation.... Our defences have been criminally neglected.... I say it with shame.... Our responsibility too.... Happily there is yet time....'

The cheering had reached its summit, could not conceivably become any louder. Or if it did become louder it would cease to be cheering, would cease even to be a noise. It would change into something else, might take on a tangible or visible form. And this in fact was what seemed to happen. The marquee became darker, as though it were slowly filling with a dark odourless smoke, and this smoke pressed upon the tutor's body, seemed to lift him slightly above the ground. For a moment he was falling, was absolutely without support, more helpless than an abandoned baby; then his feet came down on to the grass again. Noise reasserted itself – though now it had an entirely new quality. It was still cheering, was quite as loud as before, but it no longer arose from a visible source. The people in the marquee had grown calmer, were listening. The cheering came from outside the marquee – at first from immediately outside the main entrance. Gradually it decreased there, was taken up by remoter voices. However, the volume of noise did not dwindle – because now far more people were cheering. Thousands, tens of thousands. The sinister enthusiasm was spreading to the more distant parts of the racecourse. Hundreds of thousands were acclaiming the M.F.H. There were no dissentients, or if there were they would soon by lynched. A quarter of a million, perhaps more, were ready to believe whatever the M.F.H. or Tod or Silcox chose to tell them. Men and women of all social classes. The pest would spread far beyond the racecourse, had without doubt begun to spread already. A desert of limitless ignorance surrounded the tutor. A desert of danger. He knew that the M.F.H.'s story of a plot was a lie, the story of an immediate external threat was a lie; but he knew too that violence was much nearer to him than it had been before; now it was rapidly approaching. It might break out at any moment – visibly, tangibly, in one form or another. Audibly – a noise of reconnoitring aeroplanes, the bawling of sergeants. But not yet. The noise at present was nothing more than cheering. Louder it grew, straining to mount beyond the highest peaks of sound.

Darkness pressed in upon him once again, lifted him. Horror of the future alone supported him, kept his consciousness alive. He would be gassed, bayoneted in the groin, slowly burned, his eyeballs punctured by wire barbs. Yet it was not the thought of these physical agonies that really horrified him. He was unable to imagine them vividly enough. And such extremes of torture could not last long, could not compare in persistence with the other slower horrors which he *was* able to imagine. The horror of isolation among a drilled herd of dehumanized murderers. The death of all poetry, of all love, of all happiness. Never more to be allowed to use his brain. Lucky the men who got killed at once, at the very beginning of the war, before the world had reached this stage of slavery. But perhaps this stage would come first, would precede the war; perhaps it had come already. It had come, it was here, was in the marquee. They were mobilizing. Gone for ever was his hope of making friends, of establishing contact with human beings. There were no human beings. He was isolated among brutal slaves. Nothing remained for him except to try to live in his imagination. But he would not even be allowed to do that. They would seize him, mobilize him. He would be drilled, given no rest, bawled at or kicked whenever he tried to begin to dream. They were coming for him now. The young men had broken their ranks, were dividing into groups. Darkly he saw them, some of them filing out through the main entrance, others moving forward among the crowd inside the marquee. They were searching for someone. They were advancing towards him. All at once he lost sight of them completely. Strain his eyes as he might he could not locate them in the darkness. Nevertheless he knew with certainty that they were rapidly approaching him. At any moment one of them might touch him, might come up from behind and catch him by the elbow. In panic he swung round to look behind him, saw no one.

Madly he began to run.

Nobody opposed him, no foot shot out to trip him up. He raced towards the side entrance. The ticket seller sitting at the table took no notice of him. The tutor plunged out into the sunlight. He stumbled over a tent peg, only just regained his balance. Darkness had disappeared. There was no noise out here, not a hint of a sound of cheering.

He stopped running.

3

In a daze he began to walk. The sun was bright and there was no noise at all. There were no people. Wrong; there was someone walking away from him, in the opposite direction. Someone who might have come out of the marquee at the same time as he had. A man; short, hatless, wearing a black overcoat. Strangely, the tutor didn't feel in the least afraid, didn't suspect that he was being shadowed. On the contrary he had a feeling of security; and this wasn't merely because the man was walking away – it was because there was something sympathetic, almost friendly about him. The tutor glanced towards him again, but he had gone. Where? How? The tutor felt cheated. He had badly wanted to have another glimpse of him. And now he knew why – because the man had had an extraordinary resemblance to himself, had worn exactly the same sort of clothes, had had the same kind of face and figure. But all this was simply a delusion. The events in the marquee must have affected his mental health. He would have to be very careful; if he lost control of his thoughts, if he became really insane, he would be finished for ever. He must regain control, face what had happened during the last half hour. He remembered the marquee, and his new feeling of security was finally destroyed. Where was he going now?

He was going away. To escape from people, because people meant death for all that he wanted and admired. The happy, innocent, gentle, generous life – this could not exist among them. Perhaps it could not exist anywhere at all. Consider the possibility calmly: suppose that sort of life were a hallucination, a mirage.

What would remain? Nothing. A gap. A huge crevasse. But feeling would not cease to exist; it would become gradually, agonizingly, colder. And the colder it became the greater would be the agony. His heart walled round with ice. Walking seemed more of an effort than it had before. But he must walk. Never give up. Fight to think out this problem. How, even now, to learn to live the desirable life. Never to abandon that hope, so lovely, so brilliantly convincing in its emotional power. It could not be a fraud. He had made the mistake of trying to realize it among people. Now he knew better. If that life was to be found at all it must be looked for in solitude and in imagination. He would go and live in a country cottage, by himself. Possibly he could induce MacCreath to offer him a cash allowance in lieu of a job. Don't consider the details. Imagine the cottage. He would arrive there. Then the life would begin – day after day after day. Innocent walks, reading, contemplation, poetic dreaming. What about food? Don't consider that now. He would at least have money to buy it. But tradesmen would call; or worse, he would need to go into shops in the village for it. He wouldn't be able to avoid dealing with people. Don't consider – besides, he could grow his own food. Could he? No, he wasn't Thoreau. As a matter of fact he was exceptionally helpless, unpractical. He would have to go into shops, would have to make contact with one or two people. And those people would be in contact with other people who would be in contact with wider circles outside the village. News would come through to him, rumours, warnings. More; fashions, opinions, modes of behaviour, politics, would invade the village from outside. Ultimately he would be no better off than if he had chosen to live in town. He would be worse off – because he would be more conspicuous. War preparations, tyranny, torture, would invade the village, and he would have no more chance of escape than a rabbit who has been singled out by weasel. There was no escape. The happy life was a fraud.

An icy vacancy remained. Walking was becoming more and more difficult. A freezing cramp tortured his legs and arms. He dared not stop. If he did he would freeze to death. No, not to death – he would not be as fortunate as that. His consciousness would continue to live, intolerably constricted, concentrated into an atom of agony, pricked and pressed upon from all sides by microscopic needles of ice. But there must be a way of escape. If only he could think of it in time. Deliberate death. Suicide. The idea made him feel a little better. He would not become insane, lose all control. He would destroy himself. How? Don't consider the details. But unless he considered them he would not be able to convince himself he was really going to do it. He would first of all have to buy a gun or a revolver. Preferably a revolver. Then the licence. Would the police believe him when he told them he wanted to shoot rabbits? Very well, consider an air rifle. Too clumsy. An air pistol. It wouldn't be powerful enough. Suddenly he had solved the problem. He would buy an air pistol, travel down to the seaside, hire a boat, row well out to sea. He would stand facing the side of the boat, so that when he had shot himself he would fall forward into the water. He would shoot himself in the temple, be stunned instantly, would be drowned without knowing what was happening. Painless as wishing. He would do it on his birthday. He felt almost exhilarated. The pain had gone from his arms and legs and he was walking now with hardly any effort. The problem was solved. Once again he began to believe that the desirable life was possible for him. But wasn't there a contradiction here? Death and life. If the prospect of living was no longer intolerable what was the point of killing himself? Suppose he didn't kill himself. Then sooner or later he would arrive back at the state of unbearable misery from which his idea of suicide had originated. On the other hand if he did kill himself the desirable life would be lost to him for ever. But he knew he wouldn't kill himself. When the time came he wouldn't dare, would be too weak. The idea had been nothing more than a daydream, a consolation. It was already beginning to abandon him. He was slipping back into the crevasse.

Ice was closing in upon him. More painful than ever became the effort to walk. The freezing cramp renewed in his legs and arms, began to extend to his chest and to the small of his back. Soon he would lose all power of resistance, go mad. Horrible thoughts, diseased images, sickening sounds, would gain unrestricted mastery over him. But there was one last chance of escape. To turn back towards the marquee. To make one final effort to identify himself with those people. Surrender all his romantic demands, become a hopeless slave. He could not go on, go forward. Vacancy, a huge crevasse, was in front of him. He could see nothing, not even the ground that was directly beneath his feet. An icy-cold mountain mist confronted him. He turned. He saw the grass. Then he saw the marquee – quite clearly. But as soon as he tried to move towards it he realized that his legs were dead, devoid of feeling. Life, an agonized life, existed somewhere – not down there. Feeling had been driven up into the middle of his body, into his bowels, into his stomach. If he wanted to move at all the movement would have to begin from the muscles here, from the agony here. He made a terrible effort, looked down, and saw that he had lifted one of his feet a few inches above the grass. He looked ahead: the marquee was no nearer than it had been before.

He shut his eyes. Terror suggested a device to him: he would imagine a line drawn on the grass in front of him and would try to step over that. He opened his eyes, imagined a straight line of grass blades. He exerted his muscles to the utmost. With aching, horrifying labour – as though he was lifting some huge external weight – he moved his foot a few inches forward. Now it was directly above the imagined line. The descent should be easier. He foolishly looked up for a moment at the marquee. It was at least a hundred yards away. And after his foot had descended he would have to lift the other one. But at the same moment he saw something else which prevented these thoughts from developing to their conclusion. A man was passing quite close to him, walking easily and in the opposite direction. The tutor's double, the man he had seen soon after he had come out of the marquee. The meaning of this appearance was plain. The tutor was on the point of going mad. At all costs he must persist in trying to move forward. No matter if he never got anywhere near the marquee. The effort, however agonizing, would at least give him a sense of control, of power to put up some kind of resistance against the forces of boundless horror. He saw that one of his feet had descended, had reached the ground. Now to begin to try to raise the other foot. But first he must imagine a new line. No; the line was already there – a clearly defined ridge of thick dark grass, crossing his intended path at right-angles. He fought to lift his foot even higher. He looked down and saw that he still had not shifted it an inch. He was slowly freezing. Particles of ice were whirling brilliantly through the air. The marquee – though he did not seem to have moved his gaze from the grass – became visible to him. It had a flat and brittle look, as though it had been painted on a screen of glass or ice. And the row of black fir trees on the slope behind it could have been shattered to fragments by the touch of a finger. A glacial panic tightened round his heart. He could not do anything at all, could not even move his eyelids. He was done for, paralysed, a hopeless failure. He had become insane.

Suddenly he surrendered, gave up trying to move. An infinite relief, a blissful vacancy, expanded within him. Like a patient on an operating table who has been struggling frantically against the suffocating ether, he was at last anaesthetized. No need to worry about anything any more.

Now nothing existed. But out of nothing something was born. A noise, a voice. Ghostly and distinct, it came from high among the fir trees. It spoke into his ear. It said:

'...But you *are* walking. You have not failed.'

He answered it:

'I cannot move an inch. I am frozen. I am paralysed.'

'...You are walking away from the marquee. You are going towards the far end of the racecourse.'

'That's only a hallucination. I'm frozen stiff and I've become insane.'

'...No; though if you really believed that you were paralysed you would certainly be hallucinating. But you don't believe it. You can see perfectly clearly that your feet are moving and that you are walking along within a few yards of the outer white railing of the racecourse.'

'It looks as though I am.'

'...You know you are. You cannot pretend you have forgotten your black-overcoated double who went away from you soon after you rushed out from the marquee, and when you were agonizingly and futilely struggling to get back there he walked

111

easily past you in the opposite direction. You know very well who he was. He was you. He is you. He was never an hallucination. Actually you have not stopped walking since you left the marquee, and your belief that you have become a frozen paralytic merely proves you are still under the influence of the horrific delusion you hoped you were escaping from as you plunged out into the sunlight.'

'Then I am sure I must be insane.'

'...No. You are already a little saner than you were two minutes earlier.'

'But if I am any less insane than I was how is it I can hear this voice speaking out of the trees?'

'...Listen more carefully. The voice is not coming from the trees. It isn't really a voice at all. It is nothing more than a noise. A noise in the ear you had an operation on a few months ago.'

'It might be.'

'...Cast your mind back to what happened before you set out for the races this morning. Don't you remember the ringing in your ear as you followed Mr Parkin and MacCreath out of the hall towards the car?'

'Yes. But even supposing the voice is a continuation of that ringing, how am I to explain why I hear it now as words?'

'...You don't *hear* the words. They are not audible to you physically as the ringing is. They are part of an internal dialogue you are carrying on with yourself. This could be a perfectly sane and effective way of discovering the truth about yourself, if you want to discover the truth and not merely to find plausible arguments in favour of your delusory preconceptions.'

'It could be a symptom of a classic type of incurable madness.'

'...That's improbable. There are obvious differences between your case and the worst type of splitmindedness. For one thing, your first delusions were voluntary – you deliberately induced them in yourself while you were looking out of the window of the car before arriving at the races.'

'I don't see why the voluntariness of my delusions should make my madness any less likely to be permanent.'

'...You are failing to take account of how often you lapsed back into normality or near-normality from this "madness" you had such difficulty in bringing about to begin with. You are already lapsing back from the latest and most dangerous phase of it.'

'Which is that?'

'...Your attempt to return to the marquee.'

'Why was it the most dangerous?'

'...Because possibly if you had persisted in it – if, in spite of the pain and the freezing, you had forced yourself to step over the dark line of grass blades you imagined in front of you – then you would no longer have been on the border between sanity and insanity; you would have become genuinely and finally mad.'

'What ought I to do now?'

'...Stop thinking that what you see around you might be delusory. Face up to the actuality; but don't expect that the final normalizing of your wilfully deranged hearing and seeing will be easy or painless. You may suffer from withdrawal symptoms. What you have been doing to yourself is very similar to hallucinogenic drug-taking. The wilful mind can be as potent as any drug.'

'Even the worst withdrawal symptoms would be preferable to the horror I shall be escaping from.'

'...Don't be too sure of that. However, you must put it to the test. Look around you. Become aware of your real situation.'

'I am looking.'

'...What do you see?'

'People standing in front of the white outer railing of the racecourse. There are a few thousands, not hundreds of thousands, of people. The racecourse is much less vast than I thought it was. I see a bookmaker standing on some kind of platform. A woman is showing him a ticket. Perhaps the first race is finished already.'

'...Good. You are getting down to the facts at last. You are almost normal again.'

'It doesn't interest me.'

'...It will interest you. Examine the facts a little further. What do you think you will see next?'

'There will be other races.'

'...And after that?'

'The races will come to an end. People will begin to disperse.

Some of them will go towards the car park. That's where I shall go. I shall see the car that brought me here. I shall see Mr Parkin and the boy.'

'. . . Fine. Now you are facing it. And next?'

'The return. The house with the four lawns. Bed. Tomorrow. The window and the treetops. Rooks. Beer. Latin and Scripture. The day after tomorrow and the day after that.'

'. . . There's your real situation.'

'No, no, I can't stand it. So slavish, so mean. Such a contemptible apathy. It isn't life at all.'

'. . . What can you do about it?'

'Escape. In any way I can. Escape into madness even, but it would be a new kind of madness. This time I would make sure of never losing control over the delusions I would deliberately create, and they would be delusions of beauty and joy and truly requited love.'

'. . . You would not be able to control them. The problems you might have been able to solve in actual life would penetrate your delusions as horrific apparitions which you would be totally unable to escape from.'

'I don't see why this should necessarily happen.'

'. . . It would happen because you would not be able to make a deliberate choice of the type of madness you would develop. Your type would almost certainly be dementia not mania. But even if you turned out to be an ecstatically elated manic type you might not be wholly insensitive to the kind of treatment you as a mental case would get in a society which you had already found menacing while you were still sane.'

'So there isn't anything at all I can do to make my life tolerable.'

'. . . Yes, there is. But to start with you've got to recognize that your problems cannot be solved in the mind alone. Nor can they be solved in the heart, in the emotions, alone. They must be dealt with primarily in the external world. You must take living practical action. You must make use of the practical possibilities of your real situation. Are you aware of those?'

'I think I am.'

'. . . What are they?'

'To go on living in the same way as before. To be a tutor. To serve the Parkins. Or perhaps to leave them and to serve someone else. There is no other way.'

'...There is another way.'

'I suppose I might get a different kind of job. My conversation with MacCreath may not have been altogether imaginary. He may in fact feel well disposed towards me, want to do me a good turn. If I cultivated him he might eventually introduce me to someone who might introduce me to someone who might offer me a paid sinecure which would allow me plenty of leisure.'

'...It isn't utterly impossible.'

'Or MacCreath himself as an anonymous well-wisher might put money into a trust which would provide me with an assured small income just sufficient to keep me alive and completely free to follow my own bent.'

'...You don't ask for much, do you? Nevertheless if you did actually acquire a guaranteed small work-free income, you in your petty way – without having to dirty your hands with practical matters as you would have to if you were an entrepreneurial capitalist – would be profiting from the exploitation of the working class here in this country and of the oppressed and starving millions in the colonial world. You would be getting your money indirectly from the manufacture of poison gas and all the latest deadliest armaments, and you would be helping to bring nearer that extremity of tyranny and murder which your delusions in the marquee made you fatalistically foresee as inevitable.'

'Someone else told me almost the same thing earlier this morning.'

'...That does not make it any less true.'

'I remember: I imagined it. I imagined Ann told me. And I suggested to her that we should go at once together to Reykjavik or Honolulu or Ecuador or London without any preparations, without taking even a tooth-brush with us. Now I understand why I had a feeling later on while I was being humiliated by Humphrey Silcox's fiancée that I had heard the same thing said not long before about Reykjavik as she was saying to me.'

'...Be careful. You are trying to evade the issue again. The fundamental issue you ought to have faced long ago. Let us admit that your conversation with Ann was largely imaginary. She may or may not actually hold the opinions which you imagined she said she had got from you. The point is that you do hold them, have held them for some time, though since becoming the Parkins' tutor you have let yourself forget them. The ideas she seemed to express are in fact your own.'

'What good have they ever done me?'

'... You have never tried to put them into practice.'

'I suppose I have thought that, for me, they were impracticable. I am a tutor in a reactionary household. I am isolated. There is no way out.'

'... There is a way.'

'Where?'

'... You know where.'

'Yes, I know where.'

'... The way of the Internationalist Movement for Working-class Power. You should get in touch as soon as possible with the British Section of the Internationalists. But don't give notice immediately to Mr Parkin. You must think up some inoffensive and convincing reason – for instance, that you have received a sudden offer of a job in the film industry which you have been hoping for a long time to get – and you must give notice very apologetically and with a semblance of the greatest regret. Remember you will still have to earn your living after you contact the Internationalists and you will probably have to do so in education of some kind and a bad reference from Mr Parkin would not help.'

'Is there nothing I could do for the Internationalists before I leave the Parkins?'

'... You could talk with the local schoolmaster and the Congregationalist Minister. It is improbable that they like Mr Parkin. They can hardly be unaware of the low opinion he holds of them, so you might find them ready to give a sympathetic hearing to socialist ideas. And you could also go and see Ann MacCreath. She too might be sympathetic.'

'My fear is that when I do actually meet with Internationalist members they may not want me in their movement.'

'...They will want you.'

'But my upbringing, my education, my social origin – won't these tell against me?'

'...Others from your social class have been accepted before you, and have become loyal and exemplary fighters for the cause. And its founders were themselves of bourgeois origin.'

'I cannot believe that I would be accepted. My insanity would tell against me.'

'...Why are you forgetting your discovery that it is possible for you to return from your recent "madness" to normality or near-normality? It's time you stopped trying to think up reasons for expecting to be rejected by the Internationalists and decided once and for all to give yourself whole-heartedly to supporting the cause of the international working class. And your best hope of becoming as sane as you are capable of being will be by putting your political work first always instead of preoccupying yourself continually with improving your state of mind.'

'But have I the courage to take the first step? To knock on the door, introduce myself to the group secretary, ask what work I can do?'

'...It wouldn't require much courage. At worst they might take one look at you and tell you politely that they didn't need you. However, you know they won't do that.'

'I know. Nevertheless for me it would require courage. It would be such a plunge in the dark.'

'...Not in the dark. You would not be ignorant of where you were going.'

'I would not be ignorant. But I would be aware that my life was about to undergo a complete change. Yes, there's the crux, there's the root of all my remaining misgivings. I would be aware that joining the Internationalist Movement would teach me to fight against the things in my life I have helplessly loathed and feared; but might it not also destroy the things I have valued and loved?'

'...What things?'

'I cannot easily explain. Poetic dreams. The splendour and the joy.'

'...Dreams of escape. Twisted fantasies. Unhealthy substitutes for the action you ought to have taken.'

'Quite true. But they were something more than that. They may have been substitutes for practical action, but at the same time they were themselves a form of action. They may have been fantastic but they contained within themselves something other than fantasy. Unreality was not their essence; it was foreign to their essence, a taint, a disease that had invaded them. They were my attempt to find a significance in the life I was leading, to build up my experience into a coherent, a satisfying pattern.'

'... They failed. They failed because the life you were leading could never be satisfying, and consequently your attempt to build a coherent pattern was bound to result in a lie, a fantasy.'

'But surely it was better than doing nothing, was a sign of life, was better than allowing myself to sink back into apathy? The effort to understand the world, to arrive at the intellectual and emotional truth about real happenings, can never, even if it fails entirely, be worthless.'

'... In your circumstances it was almost worthless.'

'But if I am not allowed to dream or to give my time to thinking at all I do not want to live.'

'... You will be allowed – you will be expected – to dream and to think.'

'Joining the Internationalists will mean hard practical work in addition to the work I shall have to do for a living. It will mean keeping my nose down to a hundred minor jobs which in themselves and by themselves would have very little interest for me. It will leave no time for any but the crudest kind of thinking and feeling.'

'... You are quite wrong. Though it's true that you will have to make a complete break with your former thoughts and feelings. You will have to move out of the region of thinking and feeling altogether, to cross the frontier into effective action. For a short while you will be in unfamiliar country. You will have taken your so-called "plunge in the dark"; but you will not be in the dark for very long. Out of action your thinking and feeling will be born again. A new thinking and a new feeling.'

'But what will they be like in their new form?'

'... They will bear a certain hereditary resemblance to the earlier thoughts and feelings from which they were descended.

Yet at the same time they will be different, entirely new. They will be more vigorous, more normally human, less tortured and introspective. They will be concerned first with the world outside you and only secondarily with yourself.'

'How long will it be before I can contact the Internationalists? And how can I best set about contacting them?'

'...You could go to the nearest newsagent who stocks their daily paper, and you could discover from this the address of their Headquarters, and then ask to be put in touch with their nearest Branch.'

'And where would I be likely to find that newsagent?'

'...In the mining town you can see distantly from here. You can go there today, this evening – or earlier if you can catch a bus that would take you there from somewhere near the racecourse. At worst you could walk the whole way. Some newsagents stay open pretty late.'

'But unless I want to get the sack from my job as a tutor – and it would be the sack without a testimonial – I shall need to go and find Mr Parkin now and before finding him I must think up some colourable reason for telling him that I would rather not return to the house in the car and that I might not arrive back till late this evening.'

'...It won't be easy. But what about explaining that the countryside as you have viewed it from the racecourse has looked so attractive that you would like to explore it on foot? He might not object to that – not if you have the courage to insist.'

'Suppose he continues to object in spite of my insisting?'

'...You must continue to assert yourself against him. It is an essential first step. You must redeem your cowardice of this morning when you failed to refuse to go to the races. His complete surrender to Stokes after Stokes had made him furious for a while should help you to feel at least a little confidence that he might give in to you if you don't give in to him.'

'I'll try it.'

'...And if by any chance you arrive back very late – very late indeed, perhaps as late as the following morning – you could say very apologetically, that you had lost your way in the dark.'

'I feel now that whatever the risks may be I need to set about

contacting the Internationalists without a single day's delay, if
that's possible.'

'...It is. And you had better get going at once. You may not
easily find Mr Parkin. He could be almost anywhere on the
racecourse.'

'If it takes time to find him I shall at least be able to look
around at the people here. I expect there will be miners from the
town among them.'

'...Be careful. If you catch yourself beginning to think you've
found a member of the Internationalist Movement here you
must alert yourself quickly to the likelihood that you have had a
relapse, gone back to delusions.'

'I shall not go back to delusions. I have learnt my lesson.'

'...Where are you walking?'

'I am walking near the outer white railing of the racecourse.
People are standing in front of it.'

'...Very well. You know the danger.'

'I do.'

The crowd stood three- or four-deep in front of the railing. At
rare intervals they were bunched into dense groups, or were dif-
fused so that gaps appeared among them. Rather more people
were here than, in his continuing awareness that the multitudes
he had previously seen had been a delusion, the tutor expected
to find on the racecourse in actuality. However, having recovered his sanity at last, he must take care not to fall into the opposite error of belittling the reality that surrounded him now. The
huge white marquee had been a fake, but the real marquee upon
which the fake had been based was something more than a small
grey tent. It was an ordinary medium-sized refreshment tent.
And the crowd who were not inside it were an ordinary crowd of
racegoers, neither a small nor an immensely large crowd.
Neither fashionably elegant nor dirty. Normal people, sane and
unpretentious. A few were walking, going perhaps towards or
away from the bookmakers or looking for a better position from
which to watch the next race. The majority showed not much

movement, except of hands and faces. They were chatting, peering, nodding, calling. He was sane, had entirely recovered. He had put a stop even to his harmless internal dialogue. He must avoid any kind of thinking or feeling which was in the remotest degree abnormal. He must move out of the region of thinking and feeling altogether. He must act, go in among the people.

He quickly found himself among them, in front of the white railing. He stood still. No one peered at him. He was neither welcomed nor treated as an intruder. The people near him went on chatting as before. Nevertheless he was not ignored. He had the impression that they were conscious of his presence and did not resent it at all. There was a feeling of friendliness in the air. He warned himself that feelings ought not to be allowed to invade him quite so soon after he had moved out into the region of action. There should be an intermediate period, a dreamless and fallow period. But he could not resist the happiness he was beginning to feel. He believed he was among people who were mainly working-class, who had many of them experienced life at its hardest and in spite of this were capable of being generous and tolerant. They did not try to appear remote and superior. They would not despise him for any oddness they might detect in him.

Why not dare to be glad? No, not yet. He had learnt his lesson. First he must get in touch with the Internationalist Movement. Workers were here, but the Movement was not. He was on a racecourse. He had taken no action beyond mingling with the crowd here, was not justified in beginning to feel glad. Quick, check the feeling. Be austere. Yet even the fear of losing his new sanity did not make austerity easy for him. The sun, the friendliness in the air, the knowledge that there were workers in the crowd around him, all tempted him to be glad. And there was another difficulty: he was conscious of an urge to speak to a young man who was standing near him, who was looking at him and who might be working-class. Don't speak. Don't return the look. Try to feel indifferent. But this was ridiculous. The tutor need not shut his eyes to what was actually going on around him. To shut his eyes, to become deliberately blind, would be no less dangerous than his earlier wilful attempts to derange his other senses had been. Very well then, respond to the young man's look. But remember where you are, and keep a hold over your imagination.

The young man was hatless, wore baggy plus-four breeches and a dark suede-type jacket with a zip-fastener at the neck. There were large diamond-shaped bright red and canary coloured checks on his stockings. His style of dress, however, did not give an impression of showiness or of bad taste. The loud colours and the assertive bagginess were mellowed by wear and weather, though nowhere to the point of dinginess or shabbiness. He had close-cut yellow hair, and his complexion was evenly and palely red. His eyes were light blue, and they looked at the tutor with friendly interest. Suddenly, easily, he spoke to the tutor.

'You've been lucky.'

'How?'

'My mistake, perhaps. I thought you might have picked a winner.'

The tutor did not ask what made the young man think so. 'A horse? No, I haven't. As a matter of fact I didn't put anything on.'

He at once wished he hadn't said this. It might sound as if he was a disapprover of all betting. But the young man was not repelled, said:

'I don't bet all that myself. Only now and then when I have a day at the races, and I mostly back the wrong horse. I haven't had any luck with the first race today. That's what comes of reading the tipsters in the paper. Best way is to shut your eyes and have a jab at the names with a pin. It's a mug's game really, I suppose.'

The tutor couldn't help guessing there might be something out of the ordinary about this working-class young man, who – still giving no sign of suspecting the tutor be opposed to betting – now went on:

'I didn't think the day before yesterday I'd be up here today. I usually go cycling on Saturdays with my friend who works at the same place as me, but he wanted to come to the races instead and I agreed. Now he's had a lucky win on the first race. He backed an outsider, so he's gone to find his bookie and has hopes of big money.' The young man grinned.

The words 'works at the same place as me' had excited the tutor more than he immediately realized. He would have liked to ask what the work was, but he was afraid of appearing inquisitive. Nevertheless he risked an indirect approach:

'Do you find you get much time for cycling?'

'Weekends. In the winter it's not very good of course, but in summer we often do a hundred miles or more, taking tents with us; I'm fond of camping.' Wryly smiling, the young man added:

'There's only one snag in it – knowing that you'll have to get back to the workshop on Monday morning.'

'The workshop –' the tutor began. This was almost too interesting to be true. He hoped he was not allowing himself to begin to fall back into delusions. No; he knew he was perfectly sane still. Calming himself he dared to ask:

'What does that mean?'

'The workshop is the name given to it by our Boss.'

'What sort of work do you do in it?'

'Manufacturing lampshades. They have hand-painted designs on them which are done by the Boss. These are what make the shades very profitable – to him. He's a bit of an artist. We just manufacture the shades themselves.'

The tutor became bolder:

'Do you work long hours?'

'Any hours I spend at work are long.' The young man laughed. 'But they aren't as long as in other workshops and factories I know of. And we get Saturdays off.'

The tutor was aware of feeling a disappointment which he quickly suppressed.

'Is the pay good?' he asked.

'Not bad – it's slightly above the average rate.'

'Is the workshop a large one?'

'No. It's not large, but only seven of us work there – or eight if you include our Boss.

The young man showed no surprise at the tutor's questions, did not seem to think him impertinent. And now a more audacious line of inquiry suggested itself to him. He did not try to hide his eagerness as he asked:

'Do any of the seven of you belong to a trade union?'

'Yes, we all do.'

The tutor realized he'd been hoping the young man had one of those benevolently dictatorial small bosses who insist that their employees should not join a union. An emotionally unstable social-theorist of very recent growth, without any experience of what it was like to work in a 'workshop' or factory, the tutor would have been impudent enough to try to tell this working-class man what to do at his workplace. He felt humbled now before the friendly gaze of the young man who said without any suspicion at all of what had been going on in the mind of the tutor:

'All of us had to agree to join the union before our boss would take us on at his workshop.'

The tutor tried not to show how startled he was by this. He asked:

'Why does he want you to join the union?'

'He isn't a usual sort of boss,' the young man said. 'He belongs to the Internationalist Movement.' Astonishment made the tutor incredulous:

'The Internationalist Movement for Working-class Power?'

'Yes, he belongs to it. That's a fact. Me and my friend were at an Internationalist meeting with him last night.'

This time the tutor quite failed to hide his amazement and he blurted out,

'Are you an Internationalist member?'

'Me?' The young man laughed. 'No, I don't hold with it, nor does my friend. We just went because our Boss invited us. We shan't go again.'

The tutor's dismay now at discovering that the young man disapproved of the Movement was offset by the thought that he ought not to expect to meet an Internationalist on the race-course. If he had met one he could not have been certain that he wasn't up to his old fantasy tricks again. And there was another thing which blunted, which entirely neutralized his dismay. An interesting face, a face that he recognized, had appeared among

124

the crowd. It was the face of Ann MacCreath. She too was talking to a young man, and he looked like a worker. Perhaps the tutor's conversation with her in the open touring car had not been altogether delusory. She might in actual fact have become interested in the Internationalists. He remembered she had asked him a number of questions about them once when she and Dorothy with their parents had come to visit the Parkins and she had sat next to him slightly apart from the others. Certainly he didn't intend to let himself imagine that she had become a really active helper of the Internationalist Movement; but perhaps she had made a beginning, had gone farther than he had. She might already have got in touch. Or perhaps it wasn't impossible that as an actual fact she had gone very much farther than this. She might even have been accepted as an Internationalist member.

'They are beginning to line up for the next race,' the tutor's young worker said. There was pleasure in his voice. He added:

'Just time to go and put a little something on. Are you coming?'

'Well, I don't think I will, not yet.'

'All right.' He looked mildly into the tutor's eyes. 'See you again later.'

As he turned and began to walk away his face seemed to show that he had already forgotten all about the tutor. His interest had turned wholly in another direction – but the change did not suggest unfriendliness. His new and final look had nothing in common with the aloofness of so many of the ruling-class people in the marquee. Potentially he was still well disposed to the tutor. Just as the crowd along the railing were well-disposed, though their friendliness had not yet actively shown itself. He must do something to deserve their friendliness, to bring it out into the open. He must do something to help the cause of the people. Ann had already begun. He would go and speak to her. He would tell her he had at last decided to act up to his opinions. Perhaps he and she would be able to work for socialism together. Then they could become lovers, though Love in itself could never be sufficient for them. If they wanted their love to survive they must always make the socialist cause their first concern.

The crowd had begun to move closer to the railing. Ann's head was still visible, but he would have to stand on his toes if he wanted to see her face. He stretched, almost jumped, caught a glimpse that showed her earnestly talking. More people were coming towards the railing. Quickly he began to move. He must get somewhere where he would not lose sight of her. He moved forward behind the backs of the crowd. A preoccupied walker, gazing towards the course, obstructed him. The tutor dodged, lightly bumped into someone else. He apologized. He looked up and saw MacCreath.

'Hullo,' MacCreath said. 'Don't let me stop you if you are in search of a bookie.'

'No, I'm not,' the tutor stupidly admitted.

'Anyway I doubt whether you would have got to him in time. The race is just about to start. Yes, look. My word, I believe they're off. Yes they are.'

He caught the tutor by the upper arm and hurried him back in the direction of the railing. The crowd completely blocked the tutor's view. A rhythmical thudding grew rapidly louder, and for a moment the ground under his feet seemed to be shaken. He saw nothing of the race except the dark blue passing top of a jockey's cap. The thudding dwindled. MacCreath somehow had seen everything.

'Won by less than half a head,' he asserted. 'Easter Egg was leading him all the way. Right up to the finish. Won't Jim Parkin be pleased.'

'What won?'

'Fritillary of course. But I was unlucky. I listened to Stokes. Won't Jim be delighted. Nothing pleases him more than to score off Stokes. He doesn't often succeed in doing that.'

MacCreath smiled significantly at the tutor, added:

'He will hardly be able to contain himself. Which reminds me – he'll be wondering where I've got to.' Again the significant smile. 'Between you and me, I was not altogether sorry to be able to tell him – quite truthfully, mind you – that I'd promised to go and look for my daughters. I'm very fond of Jim, but there are times when – well, you know what I'm referring to. Perhaps better than I do.'

The tutor said nothing. A little less intimately MacCreath added:

'You haven't by any chance seen Ann, have you?'

The tutor didn't answer. He was surprised that MacCreath had mentioned only Ann and not Dorothy. Fortunately Mac-Creath took his silence to mean that he had not seen her. 'I can't imagine where she's got to. I hope she hasn't taken it into her head to go off home. I wouldn't put if beyond her to decide at the last moment that the races weren't interesting. And I badly wanted to have a talk with her about arrangements for this evening.'

MacCreath gave the tutor a shy look, asked:

'Have you changed your mind about my suggestion?'

The tutor became alarmed. What suggestion? The offer to get him a good job. MacCreath was referring to their earlier conversation, to a conversation which had occurred while he was having delusions after his arrival on the racecourse from the car. The tutor must be losing his grip, beginning to slide back into hallucinations. The offer had been wholly improbable, fantastic, would never have been made to him on an ordinary racecourse by a man so little acquainted with him as MacCreath was. And there were other indications that the tutor had had a relapse. Something strange had begun to happen among the crowd. There was suddenly a violent stirring among them. It was rapidly spreading, and very many people were hurrying from all directions towards the centre of this extraordinary convulsion. A passionate shout went up into the bright air.

MacCreath, observing the tutor's bewilderment, added:

'I mean my suggestion about going to the dance.'

'What dance?'

'The dance in the Town Hall this evening.'

The tutor remembered that MacCreath's suggestion about the dance had been made before they had left the Parkin house and before the car journey during which his delusions had begun. So he was all right, had not had a relapse. There was no hallucination. This meant that the commotion among the crowd must also be actual, not a hallucination. Then what was it about? What were they going to do?

'Quite an informal affair,' MacCreath said. 'No need to dress yourself up. I shan't be dressing myself up.'

He had seen what was happening among the crowd, but he deliberately, genially ignored it. His look implied that it was insignificant and not quite nice; it was beneath the notice of a gentleman. The tutor's curiosity increased. Something very interesting must be happening. What? It quite probably had a connection with the race that had just finished. Fritillary had won. Perhaps the crowd disputed the decision. MacCreath had said the race was a very close thing. A new and exciting thought flashed on the tutor; Fritillary was owned by the M.F.H.

'I'm sure you would enjoy it.'

Why not? The tutor knew, as a general historical rule, that insurrections seldom began in a way that their leaders wished or expected them to begin. He did not suppose, however, that he was witnessing an insurrection now. The crowd were making a protest, demonstrating against the M.F.H. – nothing more. Their protest had not taken the usual form of a strike or a demonstration with banners; it had taken the form of truculence on the racecourse. Fritillary's win had unexpectedly been the last straw, had broken the people's patience.

'Are you coming?' MacCreath persisted.

Their passionate shout could have no other meaning. They had crudely, spontaneously begun to rebel, to hit back at their exploiters. They had begun to move to the attack against the forces of privilege and darkness, against everything in the world the tutor hated most. Against tyranny and war and mystery, against the conditions that had made him too a slave. And he was standing here and passively watching them. He had allowed himself to listen to MacCreath. But he wouldn't listen any longer. He answered MacCreath:

'No, I'm not coming.'

He looked towards the crowd and noticed that they seemed to have become less active. He added briskly:

'And if you'll excuse me, I've something I want to attend to now.'

He rudely turned and walked away.

He hurried behind the backs of the crowd towards the centre of the perturbation which had shifted and become more distant. About thirty yards in front of him, indistinctly beyond a screen of dodging heads, he saw something or someone who did not move. Whatever it was, the climax of its interest for the crowd had already passed. People no longer came running towards it from all directions, and even the dodging heads in front of him showed a decreasing eagerness to glimpse it now. Perhaps the police had arrived, the tutor thought. The protest had failed. And he had done nothing to help it. He had betrayed it, shirked his first chance to join with the workers. But possibly the protest had not failed, would within minutes rise again. Even now he might not be too late.

He ran. He swerved away from the crowd at the railing, peering at them as he ran, trying to locate some point of promising disturbance among them. There was none. Movement had distributed itself evenly along their lines, had subsided to a normal activity of heads and hands. Their faces were turned once more towards the course.

He too became normal, stopped running. The crowd had not demonstrated against the M.F.H. Or if they had they had very soon desisted, allowed themselves to be doped by a footling interest in the next race which was just about to begin. More likely their truculence had been due to an argument with a bookmaker. Or perhaps one of the spectators had quarrelled with another who had blocked his view. Or, at most, a pickpocket had been caught. Demonstration, protest – nonsense. The tutor had expected too much.

The crowd cared only for the races. He walked on behind their backs. He walked without purpose. They would never protest, provided they got the chance of being amused occasionally; and their rulers would always see that they did get it. The people would never raise a finger against injustice, against tyranny and war. They would ignorantly, willingly submit. He walked on, weak with depression.

He turned away from them. The ground in front of him sloped upwards slightly. He was going in the direction of the car park. He looked once again at the crowd by the railing. The course curved in a semicircle away from the car park. Without shock he saw, standing a few feet back from the crowd and at the point where the bend began, Mr Parkin and Donald. They were staring at the course. They did not see him. He felt no alarm or distaste – only a feeble grief, as though, in a moment of utter defeat someone had laughed at him. He walked on.

The ground in front of him gently ascended, reached its unremarkable green summit about twenty yards ahead, stretched level from that point onwards towards the car park. On the summit and a short distance away there was a small green mound. A young man was standing on this. He wore a smart black hat and his complexion was pink and girlish. He was facing the course, but there was something about his posture and expression which suggested that he was not looking at the course. He was looking beyond it; and with such a bemused intensity that the tutor turned mechanically round to discover what this young man saw.

Nothing. At least, nothing that was new to the tutor. The tableland abruptly ending, vanishing downwards towards the broad afternoon countryside. The variously coloured rectilinear fields. Broken glimpses, among hedges and trees, of the road along which he had come this morning in the car. And far off, there was a dead straight road – the long wide coast road which led away from the town. The white insulators on the telegraph poles. Pithead gear. The remote harbour. The sea – no longer dead blue. Blue in part, and in part glittering. And the air, though still almost cloudless – except towards the south – showed a strong contrast in its colours: where the sun was on the water the sky above the horizon appeared gloomy, and where the water was lustreless the sky was brilliant. To the south a single cloud was rising slowly above the line of the horizon. A cloudbank, or a fog bank, with a straight edge – minutely jagged like the sharp side of a razor seen under a microscope.

The sea was very calm. The land too was calm. Unstirring trees at the top of a steep grass slope cast distorted shadows downwards, as if reflected in water. A small ivied church, with Roman numerals on its clock-face, stood isolated among the nearer fields. The church he had seen from the car this morning. It was just the same as it had been then. It was the same as it had always been. The countryside had not changed; in its essentials it had never changed and would never change. As it had been in the beginning, so it would remain. Change was nothing more than an illusion. Men spent their lives in futile rebellion against reality, gave their energies to the struggle for a few meagre improvements, and they died in failure and wretched discontent. But, all the while, happiness and peace were theirs for the asking, if only they would realize that the material struggle, even when it was apparently successful, could never bring them contentment. Submission, resignation – these were the only happiness. 'In his will is our peace'.

The tutor pulled himself up sharply. He recognized where his thoughts were leading. But what had caused them to take this religious direction? The ivied church; and the young man in the smart black hat. The tutor suddenly remembered who this young man was: Everard Heseltine, the new curate at St Saviour's, whose high church practices had so infuriated Mr Parkin. The fact that he was high church perhaps explained why he had no scruples about visiting the races. Everard Heseltine, preacher of resignation to the Divine will. Let the oppressed of the world accept their oppression, and let their oppressors resign themselves to being oppressors (though they must be as charitable to the poor as they can afford to be). An eternity of punishment in hell awaits those who rebel. Nevertheless, the oppressed will rebel in the future just as they have in the past, the tutor thought, and a time will come when they will be victorious everywhere in the world. Heaven will never exist on earth, but a far larger proportion than now of the world's population will be happy most of the time. The pleasures promised today by the view from the racecourse, by the sunlight, by the sea, by the rectilinear fields, will no longer be a sinister mockery. It is already possible to make an end of poverty. Everyone, even the most reactionary, will become aware that it is possible. But there were men who resisted the improvement, because they were unwilling to lose the spiritual consolation that could be found in a world that was predominantly a vale of tears. And Heseltine, the tutor thought, might be one of these men.

But the tutor recognized that he himself had certainly been guilty of hesitating to join the Workers' Movement for fear that his poetic dreams might be brutalized and destroyed. He had let himself fall into despondency when he had discovered that the workers on the racecourse were not rebelling against the M.F.H. The next stage, unless he pulled himself together quickly, would be even deeper despondency, accompanied possibly by thorough-going delusions. He must act at once, drag himself out of the quag of thinking and feeling. He would not find the Workers' Movement on the racecourse, but he must begin here and now to make his first practical move towards finding it elsewhere. The one difficulty was – how would he begin? What reasonable action could he take immediately?

While his mind fumbled, his body seemed already to have solved the difficulty. He was walking down towards the section of the crowd which lined the bend in the white railing. He was walking towards Mr Parkin and the boy. The race must be over, because they were looking in his direction and away from the course. They did not see him yet. He had no idea what he would say to them. His body walked unhesitatingly on. They saw him. He came up to them.

'Hullo,' Mr Parkin said. 'Where did you get to?'

'I've been walking round.'

Mr Parkin was neither angry nor suspicious. He comfortably accepted the tutor's explanation. Behind the points of his moustache his cheeks curved in a fixed but convincing smile. Yet he had probably lost money on the last race – otherwise he would have been hurrying off to claim it from the bookmaker.

'I won ten shillings,' Donald was saying.

'I put it on for him,' Mr Parkin explained. 'On Fritillary.'

'But Daddy I told you to. I told you Fritillary was going to win. And I gave you your ten shillings back. If I'd kept it I would have made a pound.'

'Yes, yes, you told me. You earned your ten shillings all right, every bit of it.'

Mr Parkin added a very audible aside to the tutor: 'I'd have let him keep the other ten of course, but it's good for him to feel he's earned all his winnings himself.'

Mr Parkin's face had a look of calm pleasure. The tutor was depressed; he had lost the unthinking confidence his body had given him when he had been walking, and he could not make up his mind now about what he wanted to say. He had expected that the encounter with Mr Parkin would be disagreeable and dramatic, but actually it had proved to be very ordinary. There was no opportunity for heroics of any kind. He had returned to where he had started from, to the situation which had faced him in the dining-room this morning. Soon the races would be over, he would get back into the car, and next morning he would be in the dining-room once more.

'We kept your lunch for you,' Mr Parkin said agreeably.

The tutor looked down at the grass. Its green was dusty and stale, dulled by the tread of ordinary feet. He remembered his decision to make contact with the Workers' Movement, and the remembrance was stale and lifeless. He had no feelings. Why bother to get his own way with Mr Parkin? All forms of action were equally tasteless and unattractive to the tutor. He felt no urge, no genuine desire to assert himself. Nevertheless, out of sheer dull obstinacy, he would assert himself. He would do it on principle, without feeling, without satisfaction: he would do it merely because he had decided to do it. He said tonelessly:

'There's something I have been meaning to tell you. I shall be out this evening.'

He had not known he was going to say this. Surprised at his own words, he was even more surprised that Mr Parkin was not at all astounded.

'So you have decided to go to the dance.' Mr Parkin added an explanation: 'Mac was telling me all about it.'

'I am not going to the dance,' the tutor said.

Mr Parkin either did not hear him or did not believe him. 'I'll tell Stokes to take you in the car.'

'Thanks. But I shall not need the car.'

This time Mr Parkin did hear. Inexplicably, he grinned. There was a peculiar suggestion of slyness in his grin.

'Just as you like,' he said.

The tutor firmly went on:

'And I shall not be coming back to the house tonight.'

Mr Parkin made a polite objection:

'There's no need for you to stay out, you know. Even if you are late. We can leave the key under the mat.'

'No, I'd prefer to stay out.'

'Well, please yourself.'

Mr Parkin was relieved. The worst was over, he appeared to think. Probably MacCreath, when Mr Parkin was in a good humour at having won money on Fritillary, had succeeded after a long argument in calming all his fears – except the fear that the tutor might arrive late and forget to lock the front door. Now all was well. But tomorrow the tutor would show Mr Parkin it wasn't.

'I shall not be coming back with you in the car.'

Donald asked excitedly, aggrievedly:

'Why aren't you coming with us?'

The tutor ignored him. Again Mr Parkin looked sly. He seemed to wink at the tutor, who said:

'I think I'd better be leaving you now.'

Mr Parkin, almost laughing, retorted:

'I can see you don't believe in letting the grass grow under your feet.'

Observing that the tutor was already beginning to move away, he became more serious:

'Don't forget your lunch. You'll find it in the hamper at the back of the car. If I knew where Stokes was I'd tell him to get it out for you. You will have to find him ... I've no idea where he's got to. Everyone seems to be wandering off today.'

The tutor, stimulated by the faint resentment in Mr Parkin's voice, turned and left him. Mr Parkin called out:

'Have a good time.'

Yet again the suggestion of slyness. The tutor, walking away, suddenly guessed what it meant. Mr Parkin thought that he was going off to look for the MacCreath girls, that he had been promised a lift in their car, was going to the dance with them, and that he would stay the night in the MacCreath household. Tomorrow, when the tutor returned and said he had not been to the dance but in the town and had walked back, Mr Parkin would think differently. He would be hysterically angry.

Would he? He might be, though he might have reasons for hesitating to give the tutor the sack. Mr Parkin would be aware that finding a substitute would take time and that the new man might be even worse than the present one. But assuming he chose to forgive the tutor this time – as he was quite likely to do if he had no suspicion that the tutor had gone to the town for a political purpose (he certainly would not tolerate in his household anyone he discovered to be an active socialist outside it), the tutor was nevertheless determined not to allow himself to be hindered by Mr Parkin from doing political work in this district.

The tutor was passing the refreshment tent. He was approaching the road which led downwards from the racecourse. He had made up his mind what he would do. He would walk into the town. It was not more than five miles away, and he would arrive there within an hour and a half. He would visit the newsagent's shop outside which he had once seen a poster advertising a meeting of the Internationalist Workers' Movement. He would ask the newsagent to put him in touch with the local secretary of the Movement.

He would get in touch. Then he would walk back to the house, and the next morning he would begin tutoring again, but with a difference. There would be evenings when with Mr Parkin's knowledge he would go to see the village schoolmaster or the Congregationalist Minister. He would talk to them about the Movement. Mr Parkin would give him the sack if he got to hear about this. In which case the tutor would go to London, where the Movement was at its strongest. His decision to join it would not make life easier for him. But at least he would have come down to earth, out of the cloud of his irresponsible fantasies; would have begun to live. He had already begun. He had asserted himself against Mr Parkin. Nothing, no subsequent danger could cancel that.

The tutor reached the road and started to walk down the hill.